AREA FRH41:
Happy Howloween

Written by
Todd A. Hutchinson

Contents

Preface

This book is dedicated to my precious family and friends who have endured years of my overactive creative brain. For over four decades I have been scribbling words onto a page. It began with song lyrics, poems, and monologues for my high school drama class. That morphed into screenplays, teleplays, and stage plays. Every thought, character, and story idea that swam in the deep waters of my imagination itched and annoyed my mind until I was able to transfer it down on paper then computer. Every situation in life is a story, some stranger than others and it has been proven time and time again that truth is stranger than fiction. It was always my hope that I would eventually receive the courage to write a book. I always feared the structure of novels, and I was never an avid reader. My life was all about films and television, so naturally my love for writing plays flowed much easier.

This book is also an ode to those wonderful and terrible creature feature films I grew up watching in the late seventies, eighties, and early nineties. From Swamp Thing, Pumpkinhead, Alien, to Jeepers Creepers and all others in between. I love a good monster. A creature in the basement, a beast in the water, or a big foot in the forest. They all hearken back to the David and Goliath memory of all of us. Terrorized by something bigger, faster, or stranger than you, and through sheer might, luck, or divine help you overcome the impossible. I spent countless hours in the dark of the theater enjoying my popcorn and coke, hiding my face, and letting out a screech during the jump scare.

I want to give a salute and a thank you to all the great horror writers who have come before and paved the way. From Lovecraft, King, Lumley, Koontz, Rice, and countless others who blazed a trail deep and wide enough to follow. There is nothing new under the sun, and stories have been retold for thousands of years, and should continue for thousands more. I can only hope that my version is either timely, reimagined, fresh, or just desired. If this leap of faith to step forward into fiction can inspire the next writer to do the same, then all the time spent will be worth it. Each generation is tasked with inspiring, mentoring, and preparing the next generation to evolve the narrative and make their own mark.

To my wife Sandra and my son Kaleb who have always loved me and the crazy ideas I have tried to make reality. For always allowing me to attend movies, and binge watch shows, even if it wasn't their cup of tea. These stories are for you. To Deanna and Deb, the two people I trust the most, to read my first drafts. I know you will always be honest and give me lots of red markings.

To my brothers in arms Marcus, Joel, Ruby, Robert, Mr. Wardlow and Bravo, thank you for always enjoying my sense of humor and constant flow of creative ideas. I can always count on your laughter, prayers, ideas, and truth.

To the future readers this horror book series is for you. I hope it gives you the entertaining break you deserve, the creative spark you need, and the memories to be cherished. This is book one of an initial eight-part series. My hope is that the first eight will be well received and the series can continue for more books.

I now invite you into the sleepy and mysterious town of Forest River Hill, which sits quietly in the valley of The Gemstone National Forest area perfectly set in the Pacific Northwest United States. The town is picturesque, and the townsfolk are salt of the earth. A few with unique stories, and some with strange talents. For the most part the town is normal and thriving, with a great tourist business, festivals, and seasonal charm. A dark secret is looming underneath the surface, and the town's Sheriff is trying to solve her own mystery.

The story begins with the arrival of a new Deputy who brings his own secret, talents, and troubled past. He is about to encounter the challenge of his lifetime as he realizes, behind the veil of this beautiful wilderness town lies a sinister experiment happening deep in the forest. There seems to be a reoccurring problem the town and its officials are having to deal with. The town is being plagued by the appearances and disturbances of strange cryptic beings. The fables of things that go bump in the night, scratching's on walls, voices in the dark, and beings lurking in the shadows are becoming reality.

Can the Sheriff and her new Deputy find the courage, strength, and wisdom to deal with these demonic and sinister forces, while maintaining the charm of this mountainside village? What is behind these new and strange occurrences? Will the town ban together and resist this attempt to destroy their lives, or will they fold and succumb to the darkness that is slowly rolling down the mountain side?

I hope above all things that you sit back and enjoy the adventure that lies ahead of you as you discover the dark and strange secrets that lie underneath the history of Forest River Hill and the generations of townsfolk who have built it. Dive into the investigations of what is leading to the appearance of the cryptids. Awake to the knowledge and dissection of the possible genesis of the strange happenings in the forest, the fortified and secretive United States Military base known as AREA: FRH41 that lies deep in the Gemstone National Forest. Enjoy your journey!

Chapter 1: September Moon

Between the full moon and the roaring fire there was plenty of light and warmth for the Kelly's Steel Fabrication company softball team. This was a night for celebration, for they had just won their second championship in the Forest River Hill Municipal adult softball League. Their captain, and lead engineer Bill Molten had reserved the campsite at the beginning of the season, as if he were assured of their victory. They were tucked away in the high elevation of the northwest end of Gemstone National Park, inside the primitive camping site. Besides Bill, five other men, Al Thorn, Larry Brett, Matt White, Joey Marx, & Mark Roberts were able to join the festivities. They sit around the fire eating and drinking, discussing their current victory.

Bill raises his beer, "To the two-time champs!" The rest of the men raise their beer in their own way all chanting "Two-time Champs!" The men take a large swig. In the distance a faint howl echoes through the camp site and drift into the night. "Oh no, Larry, I think I hear your wife calling for you." Al Thorn gests. Larry snickers and replies, "Doubt it. She's probably in bed falling asleep watching *The Bachelor*."

Joey Marx chimes in, "I still don't know how people can watch that garbage." Matt White adds his two cents, "Works for me. While she is glued to that trash, I get to relax and watch the ball game alone." The men nod in agreement. A long howl permeates the campsite again. This time louder and longer, as if the source of that howl is getting closer.

"Sounds like she is getting close Larry." Mark Roberts remarks. Bill stands up and peers into the thickness of the trees. "Hold it down for a second boys." The boys still their chatter. Bill listens intently. A few beats later it comes again. This time the howl feels right on top of them. A few twigs snap in the forest, something approaches. The boys listen. Beers in one hand, sausage in the other. "It is deer season, maybe that howler is bringing a big ole buck our way." Al breaks the silence. Bill reaches behind his chair and grabs a rifle. He waits for another sound. Nothing but a little wind, and the usual night bugs playing their symphony. Sitting back down Bill lays the rifle across his legs. Larry, comments, "I hear they have spotted some grey wolves up in these hills lately. Some say they are getting as big as brown bears with all the food supply." "Too bad they are still protected, otherwise we could bag ourselves one tonight." Mark replies.

A loud branch snaps close by. Everyone hears it. They all get still. Bill readies his rifle in his hands. The men all look around, knowing that sound was close. The moon hides behind some clouds and the campsite becomes a little dimmer. Bill peers behind Larry, as he sees something dark moving in the trees behind him. Bill stands to his feet. Looking closer into the forest. Suddenly two glowing eyes glimmer just fifteen yards behind Larry. "Stay still boys, I think I see her." Bill silently says. He lifts his rifle and aims just over the shoulder of Larry. "Hey, hey now, Bill, careful where you point that." Larry says, moving over in his chair. The eyes fade in the distance. Bill squints to see if any other movement happens. No howl, no twigs, silence falls over the campsite. Just the crackling of the fire and the heavy breathing of the men. Bill relinquishes his aim and puts the rifle down to his side. "Sorry, Larry, just wanted to keep you safe. Probably just some stupid racoon or fox out looking for a snack." The boys give a sigh of relief, knowing the environment is prone to be scary, especially with all the sounds that happen in the deepness of the forest.

Bill chuckles for a moment. The boys all laugh, knowing how silly their fear is. Then, a bellowing growl silences their joy. Bill freezes as he realizes the growl came directly behind him. Larry, looking in terror

sees something rise behind Bill, he can barely speak out, "What in the

Holy Hell is that?" Before Bill can turn around a giant animal tackles

him. As it pushes him to the ground his hand squeezes a shot off. The

shot hits Al in the leg. Al screams. The animal, as large as a bear, but

features of a wolf is tearing into the back of Bill's neck and head, he

shrieks in pain. The other men panic. Joey instinctively tears off

running into the woods. The animal tears a huge chunk out of the back

of Bill's neck, blood spews out everywhere. Larry, knowing he brought

his gun as well, runs to his pack to retrieve it. Al tries to attend to his

leg, knowing he needs to escape. The animal looks at Al. His large

yellow eyes, and long blood covered snout pointed straight at Al. The

animal growls and reveals sharp teeth, covered in Bill's flesh. Al tries to

get up, but before he can, the animal leaps over to him, knocking him

and the chair to the ground and begins tearing into him as he screams.

Matt and Mark look around for items to defend themselves with. They

both grab logs that were waiting to be thrown on the fire. They rush

over to try and help Al, and as they approach the animal, they raise the

logs to strike it. Quickly the animal senses them, turns around, and stands on its hind legs. Matt and Mark freeze in terror. The animal stands nearly seven feet tall. It snarls and growls at them, its dark fur and wide body tower over them. Matt and Mark attempt to strike the animal. Before their logs can reach, the animal swats both of them with its two giant paws and sharp claws. Matt gets slashed across the face and falls to the side forcefully. Mark is slashed across the throat. He drops to his knees, grasping his neck as bloods pours out.

A shot blasts out, and a bullet whips past the animal's shoulder penetrating the skin. The animal turns to see Larry pointing a pistol at it. Larry attempts to fire off another shot, the animal leaps at him and takes him to the ground. This shot rips into the night and misses the animal. Larry screams as the animal tears its teeth into his flesh. The sound of grown men screaming in pain, and the snarling of the animal echo like a loud stereo in the night filling the forest with a horrific sound.

In the woods, running frantically away from the sounds is Joey. A haunting howl bellows from behind him. He gets startled and stumbles in the dark. He falls to the ground hard. He looks back into the night, toward where the campsite was and his friends. Another howl pierces the night. The sound of twigs breaking. It's coming! Joey winces in pain as he gets up and starts to run again. He is frightened. He is lost. He looks around hoping to see any sight of light and other campers. The sound of the animal running in the distance grows louder. Joey peers straight in the darkness ahead and sees what looks like a clearing. Maybe a road. He puts it in another gear and heads for the clearing. The animal gaining ground behind him. The breaking of twigs and leaves becomes closer. Joey looks behind him. A black shadow darts towards him. The flickering of the yellow eyes, like small headlights approaching quickly.

Joey directs his gaze straight, pumping his legs as fast as he can through the uneven forest ground. "Oh, God help me! Sweet Jesus, save me!" Joey prays as the clearing approaches. The animal now fixed on Joey, gains ground quickly, his loud breath rhythmic and intimidating. The animal closes in. The clearing is less than a football field away. The animal in one last effort increases its stride and closes in on Joey. Joey, unsure if he will make it to the clearing, cries out in terror. The animal, just several car lengths behind and gaining. Joey sees the opening, but it is not a clearing. It is not a road. The animal just six feet away, snaps at

Joey's heels, then extends its front paws to break as if it senses danger.

Joey, before he can decide, realizes the clearing is a cliff. He tries to

slow down but it is too late.

His body falls forward as he screams. Joey, arms, and legs flailing,

plummets thirty feet into the Thompson River below. The animal stops

at the edge of the cliff. Snarls as it sees Joey hit the water. Joey drops

into the cold flowing water. He recovers his bearings and swims to the

surface. His frightened and cold body flows downstream in the current.

The moon shines brightly over the river and cliff. Joey looks back and

up to the cliff and sees the animal perched on the edge. Its glowing eyes

watching him float away in the current. With one final statement the

animal howls to the moon. Its face and fur drenched in the blood of

the men. It takes one last look at the one that got away, turns, and runs

back into the woods.

Joey, terrified, cold, and in disbelief he was able to escape, begins to

swim with the current. He looks ahead as the river leads straight, splitting the forest in two, in the distance there is soft light. Hopefully, a campsite. Even better, the edge of town.

Back at the campsite the animal sniffs the men to see which one is still alive and which are dead. Matt, slowly breathing on the ground, terrified as the animal sniffs him. Matt closes his eyes. The animal turns and walks toward Mark who lies lifeless on the ground a few feet away. The animal grasps Mark's foot with its strong mouth. It slowly drags the body into the woods. Matt, in utter shock, passes out.

Chapter Two: The New Deputy

The morning birds sing. Cool dew glistens off the grass as the sun comes over the trees. Alice Higgins comes out onto her back porch. Her ritual of morning coffee and her classic horror novel in hand. She sits down on her rocker and places the hot coffee on the stand next to it. She peers out into her backyard, nestled on the edge of the forest. She opens her book to the last place she read. She attempts to read but hears slight moaning coming from the edge of her yard near the forest. She lowers her book and looks out. She sees something pale, sticking out on top of the grass. Her sight, not as good as it used to be. She reaches over to grab the pair of binoculars she normally uses for bird watching.

Through the lens she looks at an object, and to her dismay appears to be a naked body. She stands up quickly and lowers the binoculars. It moves in the distance. Slowly a naked man stands up, his backside to Alice. She raises the binoculars to see. Through the lens she sees a tall naked man. His body has mud and grass on it. The man looks around at his surroundings. He then turns around and sees Alice. Alice, surprised by who she sees, quickly lowers the binoculars. "Heaven's gates!" she says aloud. The man quickly runs through her yard jumps her fence and disappears into the neighbor's property.

Alice raises the binoculars and looks back to where the man was laying on the ground. Near where he was, in the grass, appeared to be an arm, severed just below the elbow. Alice lowers the binoculars. She puts her hand to her mouth in shock, the binoculars drop to the ground. She looks around, hoping her phone is on the porch but it is not. She looks down at the book she was reading, *Devils Row* by Matt Serafini, with a picture of a werewolf's claw on the cover. She grabs her coffee and hurries back inside her house.

Across the hill, in the middle of downtown, in the picturesque town of Forest River Hill, lies the historic Town Hall and Sheriff's Office. The phones are ringing. The secretary May is on the line already. "Thank you for calling. I will note what you saw and let the sheriff know." May exclaims as she hangs up the line and answers the next. "Good morning, sheriff's office, how may I help you?" May, with pen in hand prepares to write. "Good morning Mrs. Higgins." May listens. "Please, slow down. Take a breath and tell me again what you saw." May tries to calm her down.

Meanwhile inside the sheriff's office. Sheriff Mazey Keller sits behind her desk. Behind her is a wall of pictures of previous sheriffs. Sitting in the chair in front of the desk, covered with a blanket, cold and frightened still, is Joey Marx. He slowly sips a hot cup of coffee. "So, you believe it was a bear that attacked you?" Mazey asks. Joey, hands shaking puts the coffee down. "We thought it was a bear at first, but it ran like a wolf. It howled as well." Joey states. "Bill Molten and Larry Brett were found dead at the scene." Mazey remarks. "We also found a rifle and pistol at the campsite. Both had been fired," she adds. Joey, continuing to shake, answers her. "We tried to defend ourselves. It happened so fast."

Mazey looks at some papers on her desk. "Matt White and Al Thorn are recovering in ICU. Al appears to have a bullet wound in his leg. Can you tell me about that?" she asks. Joey pauses, trying to remember. "I think Al was shot when the animal hit Bill. The rifle went off when Bill was struck." Joey answers. "Larry's gun was fired twice. Can you tell me anything about that?" the sheriff inquires. Joey pauses. He grabs his coffee and drinks again. He says nothing. Just drinks and trembles.

"Reports indicate Mark Roberts was with you. He has not been found yet. Can you confirm Mark was with you last night?" Mazey asks. Joey stares back at Mazey. She could see the terror still on his face. Joey slowly nods, letting her know Mark Roberts was with them.

There is a knock on her door. Mazey looks up. "Come in!" she replies. The door opens and May walks in. "Sorry to disturb you, but the phones are going crazy, and some strange sightings are coming in from several people." May states. "What strange sighting?" Mazey asks. May takes a breath and then tells the sheriff. "Apparently there is a naked man running around the city this morning, and the town is a buzz about it." Mazey looks up at the clock on the wall that reads 7:50 am. She looks back at Joey who sips the coffee, then speaks to May. "Thanks, May, for the heads up. Call Hocho, see if he can come in this morning. Our new deputy should be here any minute. Please let me know when he arrives." "Absolutely, will do." May replies. She leaves and shuts the door behind her.

Mazey looks down at the papers on her desk and lets out a long breath. "Joey, I going to have someone drive you to the hospital so you can get checked out. I will come to visit you this afternoon once you are medically cleared. We will continue this discussion once you have had some time to warm up and get treated." Mazey stands up and walks over to the window in her office. The downtown begins to be filled with citizens walking to work, breakfast or early shopping. She looks back at Joey. "For your sake, and the men you were with, I hope you are right, and we can trace this animal who attacked you." She looks back out and sees a red Nissan Xterra 4x4 pull across the street and park.

Across the street, sitting in the parked Xterra sits a man, Paul James Weather. The truck is full of bags and boxes, multiple cups, and articles of clothing. The man looks down at his phone which shows in his maps app that he has arrived at his destination. He looks in his rearview mirror to see the sign outside the building, across the street, which reads "Forest River Hill Sheriff Department." He takes a deep breath, turns off the engine and exits the vehicle. He crosses the street and enters the sheriff's office.

May is inside typing away on her computer. She turns to see Paul enter the building. She takes notice he is a handsome and fit man, strong facial features, and thick wavy hair. Paul looks around and notices the age of the building, the strong brick features and columns, hard wood desks and features. He senses there are a thousand stories to tell about this place. "Good morning, Sheriff's office. I'm May, can I help you?" Paul turns his gaze to May and walks toward the desk. He greets May with a smile. "Good morning, May, I'm Paul Weather. Reporting for duty." May stands to her feet, excited. "Yes, good morning, Mr. Weather, the sheriff has been expecting you." May extends her hand to shake. Paul smiles and shakes her hand. "Please, call me Paul." May jokes, "Only if the boss lady allows me." Paul looks to the wall behind her and sees a picture of Sheriff Mazey Keller. "Please, have a seat. I will inform her you are here." May smiles and leaves for Mazey's office. Paul remains standing and takes a closer look at his surroundings. He notices on one of the walls a corkboard full of pictures of missing people. May returns quickly. "Right this way deputy, the sheriff will see you now." Paul turns and follows May into the Sheriff's office.

May and Paul enter Mazey's office. She is looking at pictures from the incident in the woods. "Sheriff, Paul Weather, your new deputy." May announces. "Pleasure to finally meet you, Mr. Weather. Happy to have you on the crew." Mazey extends her hand. Paul walks over and shakes it; he can see something in her face that is familiar to him. "Please call me Paul." Paul request. "Have a seat, I need to catch you up on some events this morning." Mazey replies. "May, please get a hold of Hocho. Have him meet us at the campsite around 9:30 am." Mazey requests. "Absolutely. I'm on it. Pleasure to meet you Paul, look forward to working with you. "You as well, May." Paul replies. Mazey and Paul sit.

Mazey opens a file on her desk and skims it quickly. Paul looks around her office. The pictures, the awards, the military décor. "So, you're the famous Lieutenant Commander my father used to brag about." Mazey states. "I wouldn't go so far as to say famous" Paul replies. "You did serve under his command though?" She asks. "Yes, Sheriff Keller. For two years he was my Captain. I was there when he retired." Paul remarks. "When I saw your name on the application, I remembered it. My father said he never served with a man who had more raw intuition than you." Mazey claims. "He was the most honorable man I ever served under. I'm terribly sorry for your loss." Paul expresses. "I appreciate that. Hard to believe it has been over four years now since he disappeared. After a brutal two-year search, my mother insisted we let him have a funeral service." Mazey emotionally shares. "No trace, even to this day of what might have happened?" Paul asks. Mazey pauses, she looks out the window as if she is expecting him to be right outside her office. "Hocho believes he is an Enoch. That God decided to take him to heaven for some reason." She speaks softly. Paul looks at her. He can see this is still a mission she is on. "Hocho?" Paul breaks the silence.

Mazey comes to out of her daze. "Yes, Hocho! He is our park ranger, and our tracker. He is a sixth generation Kootenai Indian. His great grandfather was a great warrior chief of their tribe. His grandfather was a medicine man and holy man" Mazey describes. "Sounds like a good man to have in an investigation." Paul replies. "You have no idea." Mazey responds. "That brings me to the case at hand. Sorry to throw you in the fire on your first day, but two men were found dead in the national park this morning, three are in the hospital recovering and we have one missing." Paul sits back, a small grin appears on his face. "Looks like I got here just in time." He remarks.

"No better way to get acclimated to this interesting town of ours." Mazey states. "Go see May, she will issue you a uniform, badge, equipment, and firearms. When you're dressed, we will see the judge and swear you in. We need to be at the park in an hour to meet Hocho. You remember how to double time soldier?" Mazey asks. Paul stands to his feet and extends his hand again. Mazey stands and shakes it. "Happy to be aboard Sheriff. Let's go solve ourselves a murder." Paul claims. Mazey responds with a small grin. "Dismissed!" Mazey orders. Paul performs an about face and exits the office. Mazey turns to look at her father's picture hanging on the wall. "I sure hope you are right about this one."

Chapter 3: Tracking a Beast

The morning sun darts in an out of the thick forest of Gemstone National Park. In a small clearing a few vehicles align the edge of the dirt road. Coming up the road is Mazey and Paul arriving in her police issued Ford F250 4x4. She finds a space among the other vehicles. The two exit the vehicle and step into the clearing. Paul looks around at the thickness of the forest. "This must be the primitive site up here." He claims. Mazey points to a small trail ahead of them. "The men were camping right up that trail. Hocho should be waiting at the site." Mazey leads, and Paul follows closely behind. They make their way through the winding small trail leading to the campsite. "Do you have many animal attacks up high in this area of the park?" Paul asks. "We have had our share of strange attacks." Mazey remarks as she pushes branches out of her way. "Once we get a better look at the site, we can determine if this was an animal, or just a bunch of drunk buddies having a disagreement."

The two come to a small clearing where the campsite is. The two bodies are bagged but laying in the spot they were found. Officer Ben

Ford and Officer Amy Hart are taking pictures and securing the scene. Mazey and Paul walk to them. Standing in the center of the crime scene looking intently at the woods is a very large man. Paul notices his stature which appears to be close to 6'5" or 6'6". Long jet-black hair, holding what looks like a small drum in his hand. He is adorned in his park ranger uniform with rifle strapped across his back. Mazey interrupts his gaze. "Hocho, so glad you can be here. Thank you for helping." Hocho turns to greet her. Paul stands as straight as he can, staring at Hocho's piercing eyes and strong facial features, his Indian heritage showing plainly. "My pleasure, sheriff." Hocho replies in his deep rich voice.

"This is my new Deputy, Paul Weather. He will be my second on this case." Mazey introduces Paul. Hocho extends his hand. "Paul, meet Hocho "Ghost Eyes" Evers. Park Ranger and the best damn tracker I have ever known." Mazey introduces Hocho. Paul extends his arm and shakes Hocho's hand. "My pleasure. I look forward to working with you." Paul claims. Hocho shakes his hand and stares deep into Paul's face, closer, more to his soul. "Good job sheriff. Looks like you found yourself a seer." Hocho remarks. "A seer you say. Good, maybe he will see who murdered these two men, and where the missing third one is."

Mazey replies. Hocho releases the handshake. "Me too!" Hocho states.

Paul continues his glance at Hocho, knowing there is a kindred spirit

between the two of them.

Mazey walks over to one of the bodies and opens the body bag. Bills

lifeless, mauled body lays still, and dried blood covers his pale flesh.

Mazey removes a pen from her jacket. She traces the claw marks on the

back of Bill's neck and shoulder. "So, tell me Hocho, are there animal

tracks leading in and out of this site?" Mazey asks. Hocho walks over to

where she is. Paul walks over to the other body bag. "There is. Strange

ones too. Also, man tracks leading away in that direction." Hocho

answers. Mazey peers to see which direction he is pointing. "Long

strides too, as if they were running fast." Hocho includes. "Toward the

river! Was Joey running for his life, and jumped in the river?" Mazey

asks.

Paul looks over Larry's mauled body in the bag. He studies the deep

slashes in his skin. "This definitely looks like an animal attack." He

states. He picks up a dark hair that rests on the wound. He investigates it. "This is too coarse to be a human hair." He replies and puts the hair in his jacket pocket. Mazey stands to her feet and walks toward the direction of where Joey fled. "Show me the tracks." She requests. Hocho walked to where she was then a few feet ahead of her. Paul stands up and joins them. Hocho kneels down and moves a few leaves covering the track. "It is a wolf mark. But much larger than I have ever seen. Much bigger than the indigenous ones at the park." Mazey and Paul kneel down to get a closer look. "Is there a wolf that you know of that could make this print?" Mazey asks. "Maybe the MacKenzie Valley. They are much farther north. They avoid humans at all cost. This track is bigger though." Hocho answers. Paul stands and looks around at the crime scene, and where the bodies are positioned. "Could the animal's presence have been a feeding, and not an attack?" He asks. Mazey stands. "What are you saying?" she asks. Hocho stands and listens. "Could there have been an altercation? The men fought and shot each other and then the animals came later and fed off the bodies?" Paul states.

"Then how do you explain Joey's story, and the other men's wounds in the hospital?" Mazey asks. Paul walks to the center of the campsite and looks at the forest around him. "Maybe they weren't all here together. What if the two men that fired at each other were here first. The others came later and walked into a pack feeding, and they tried to help their friends. Would a pack defend their food?" Paul asks. Hocho moves forward to address his statement. "They may defend against another animal, but not humans. They would flee and wait to come back if it were clear." Hocho answers. Mazey joins Paul and Hocho in the center. "Officer Hart, please take several pictures of that track and send them to me," she requests. "Yes, Ma'am!" Officer Hart replies and walks over to the track to document it.

"Officer Ford let's get these bodies to the coroner. Tell him I want a time of death as soon as possible. I also want DNA of these bodies, and the animal samples as well." Mazey requests. "Yes, sheriff." Officer Ford replies. "Hocho, meet Deputy Weather and me at the hospital after you're done. I want the three of us to get the stories of the three men who made it through this crazy night. Maybe one of them will tell the truth or make sense of this. Call me on the radio when you are on the way." Mazey requests. "Yes, sheriff. I am going to track the drag trail. See if I can find the missing body." Hocho remarks. "Good work.

Let me know as soon as you find something. See you at the hospital."
Mazey responds.

Mazey turns to Paul, "Okay Deputy, are you ready to see the house that is provided to you by the Forest River Hill Sheriff Department?" Paul, a small grin on his face, replies "I can hardly wait." Mazey pats him on the shoulder. "Don't get your hopes up. It's a good size, on a good plot of land, but it is old, creaky, and smelly." She states. "Sounds like a little slice of Heaven." Paul jokes. "Maybe so. Let's hit the road, shall we." Mazey confirms. She walks toward the trail they came in on. Paul turns to Hocho, "Pleasure to meet you, Ranger Evers." Hocho nods his head and responds. "Pleasure is mine, Deputy." Paul nods back and follows Mazey down the trail.

Hocho turns to follow the drag trail. He takes out a carved stick out of his jacket and begins to beat the small drum in his hand. He walks toward the trail, chanting in Kootenai to the beat of the drum. His tall frame slowly disappears in the thick forest.

Chapter 4: The Creek House

Mazey and Paul drive up a dirt road and come to a stone bridge that has seen better days. The bridge crosses over a flowing creek. The truck tires rattle across the uneven bricks of the bridge. Paul looks out the window at the creek, and in the distance at the end of the road an old two-story house. By the looks of it, it hasn't been lived in for a while. "It doesn't look pretty from the outside, but it has great bones, plenty of space, and five acres of peace and quiet in a picturesque mountainside." Mazey remarks as the truck survives the bridge and continues down the dirt road leading to the front porch of Paul's new abode. "Remember, I spent eighteen months on a Naval ship with only eight feet of personal space. This is a resort!" Paul responds. Mazey brings the truck to a stop and the two get out. Paul looks the property over. Plenty of trees, places to wonder. A fresh creek that runs around the property and into the mountain side. There is a feeling though that this house has been through some things. Some people. That it may have a personality of its own, and maybe even a few spirits Paul may have to contend with.

Mazey walks up the steps, onto the porch. Paul follows behind. "It has power, water, and is completely furnished." Mazey states as she reaches for a small set of keys in her pocket. "There is a good-sized generator in the basement that will keep the place going if the power does shut off." Mazey adds. She finds the key that opens the front door, creaking as it opens, and a rush of wind comes from the house, as if something were set free. Paul takes a deep breath, as if to prepare himself for what may wait inside. The two walk inside. It is dark, musty, and cold. Some light comes through windows that the curtains are open, and from a large stained-glass window on the first flight of the staircase. Mazey looks to the wall and flips a light switch, which turns on the large chandelier in the main room on the first floor.

Paul looks around. It looks rather comfortable, with large wooden furniture, side tables, bookcases, and plenty of space. It is quiet. No sign of a human for a spell, and it definitely feels unlived in. "There is a lady in town who comes and cleans it once a month, changes all the linen, and makes sure everything is working." Mazey says. Paul looks at the large fireplace and the taxidermy animal heads that adorn it. "I can have her come maybe every week, or every other week if you need her." Mazey informs Paul. "I should be fine. All the time in the military has taught me how to keep a tight ship. Plus, it's just me, shouldn't be making much of a mess." Paul responds. "Let me show you the kitchen and out back, you are going to love the view." Mazey states as she leads Paul across the main room and into the kitchen. Paul follows.

The kitchen is large, galley style, with a large island in the middle. In the far end of it is a dining area with a large table for eight. Windows behind presenting the view of the sprawling back acreage. "As you get to know the people in town, this is a good house to do some entertaining, if you're into that kind of thing." Mazey remarks as the two of them look over the kitchen. "I've been known to throw a party or two in my day." Paul responds. "It's fully stocked. All the pots, pans, plates, glasses, and utensils you need. Anything else you need, I'm sure you can find in town." Paul opens the fridge, which is completely empty, but working. "You'll probably want to make a grocery run after work today and stock up." Mazey adds. "Ready to see outside?" She leads him down the kitchen, through the dining area to a door that opens to the back porch.

The two walk outside to a huge porch, covered in rocking chairs and tables, lights that hang, and steps that lead down to a large backyard that slopes down to the flowing creek that separates the property and the forest which leads into the mountain side. Mazey stares at the expanse. Paul walks beside her and takes a gander at what will be his new view every morning. "It is really quiet out here at night, just the trickling of the creek and the sounds of the forest. Hopefully, it will give you some good nights of sleep." Mazey mentions. Paul peers closer to the creek to what appears to be a large shed or single room cabin. "What is kept in there?" Paul asks. Mazey looks, tries to remember the last time she was in there. "Mostly equipment and tools, I believe. There are some traps as well, in case you get some large visitors from the forest." Mazey responds. She hands the keys to Paul. "One of those will probably open that door out there." Paul grabs the keys. "Why don't we have a seat for a second and visit, since we have this great view." Mazey requests. The two sit down in the rocking chairs. They both look out and take a few beats, enjoying the crisp cool air and sounds of nature.

Mazey begins. "I took this job four years ago, after my father went missing. He had been the sheriff for twenty years; his father was the sheriff before him for thirty-five years. The last three generations of my family have been in charge of keeping the peace for this region for over half a century now. In the last three years I have been through eight deputies. Six of them resigned, the other two transferred somewhere else. I also got divorced and have been raising my two children." Mazey pauses and looks at Paul. He peers back, intently listening. Mazey continues. "I picked you for a reason, for several reasons really. One, you are a soldier. This job requires a trained individual. Second, your education. I know you have degrees in criminal justice, and theology. I also know you minored in parapsychology, and the paranormal." Mazey pauses for a breath. She rocks a few times in her chair. Paul keeps his eyes on her, waiting for the need to respond.

Mazey continues. "I also know about your trouble with the church group, and what happened to that girl. I don't know if you had anything to do with her death or not, only God knows that. What I do know is you paid the price for it, and you are still standing." Mazey pauses and looks over at Paul. He keeps his gaze on her. "I need someone who can face their fears. Someone who believes there is more out there than what our eyes may see. Someone who knows how to call on a higher authority when needed. We may have a small size town, but we have big mysteries, and mysterious things happening all year long." Mazey reaches into her shirt pocket and pulls out a badge. She holds it out to look at it and so Paul can see it. "This was the only thing of my father's that we found. His badge. I believe he left this for me to find. As long as I have breath, I will seek the truth and find out why this was left behind." Mazey pauses and slowly stands. Paul stands and continues to listen.

Mazey turns to him and continues. "You need to be ready. When things get hectic, know that as a marine, I will always have your back. As your sheriff, I will give you all the tools you need." She puts the badge back in her pocket. "I just need to know one thing from you. Are you ready to report back to duty, soldier?" Mazey asks, firmly looking Paul in the eyes. Paul takes a deep breath, keeping his focus on Mazey and the severity of what she is asking. He straightens himself and responds. "Absolutely, sheriff." Paul extends his hand to her. Mazey straightens herself as well, extends her hand, and the two firmly shake in agreement. "Welcome to the Forest River Hill Sheriff's Department, Deputy Weather." Mazey confirms. They both smile and release the handshake. Mazey looks once again at the view of the backyard. "It is a crazy view. Okay let's get to the hospital and question those campers, try to find ourselves a murderer or a predator?" I'll give you a few minutes to walk the place so you can get your bearings. Meet me in the truck out front in ten minutes." Mazey states as she pats Paul on the shoulder and walks back inside. Paul puts the keys in his pocket and walks inside after her. "All the bedrooms are upstairs, go claim the one you like." Mazey says as she heads to the front door. Paul makes his way up the staircase which leads to a long corridor. A large window at the end, three doors on either side evenly spaced down the hallway. He opens the first door on the left to reveal a small bedroom. He doesn't enter. He opens the door directly across which reveals another small room that appears to be used as a study. He doesn't enter. He walks to the next door on the left and opens it. It opens to a large bathroom with sinks, shower, and large tub. Across the hall the other door opens to a similar bathroom. He walks down the hall and opens the third door on the left. It appears to be another small bedroom. He crosses the hall and opens the third door on the right. This door opens to a much larger room, a large bedroom, and a room to the side with a sitting area and a large bathroom. The primary bedroom it appears. Paul walks inside to view it more closely.

Paul is happy to see it is a king size bed, tossing in his sleep requires plenty of room. The large dresser and two side tables should provide plenty of space for the minimal items he possesses. Paul walks over to the sitting area. The small bookshelf, already filled with a good selection of books. The small table with lamp and two chairs facing the large window will be a welcome comfort at the end of his long days. Paul walks to the window and peers out. In the distance is the small shed or cabin he asked about. The creek flowing swiftly behind it. He can barely make out on the other side of the creek a small trailhead leading into the forest. Perhaps an adventurous hike will be in his future he ponders. His gazing is interrupted by footsteps, as if Mazey is coming up the stairs to get him.

"Sorry, on my way. Just getting the lay of the land." Paul states as he turns himself around and heads out of the bedroom back into the hall.

The footsteps stop as he enters. Paul looks toward the stairs to see

Mazey. She isn't there. "Sheriff?" Paul calls out. He stares down the

corridor. Maybe she went to the bathroom. Paul notices as well, all the

doors he opened to each room, are now closed. He instinctively reaches

for his gun and aims it down the corridor. "Sheriff!" He announces

louder. He slowly walks down the corridor. As he passes each door, he

opens it and aims inside. No movement. No Mazey. He makes his way

to the study at the beginning of the corridor. He can hear a faint

whisper behind the door. He moves in closer, pressing his ear to the

door. One hand on the gun, the other slowly opening the door handle.

The whisper gets louder, almost audible.

"Paul! You coming!" Mazey shouts from the bottom of the stairs. Paul

was startled. The whisper stops. "Yes. Be right there." Paul responds.

He thrusts open the door. No one. Nothing in the room. Just as it was

when he first opened it. Paul takes a deep breath and holsters his side

arm. "Stupid old house." He mutters as he closes the door and walks

downstairs.

Chapter 5: He Was Tall

Mazey and Paul walk through the main doors of the Moorehouse Medical Center Hospital. Patients, nurses, doctors, and medical assistants fill the front room. Mazey leads Paul to the front desk and the lady that sits behind it. "Afternoon Carol, we are here to see patients Matt White and Al Thorn. This is Deputy Weather. He started today." Mazey announces. Carol looks at Paul and greets him with a happy smile. "Welcome aboard deputy, so happy to meet you." Carol says. Paul returns with, "Nice to meet you, Carol." Carol types on her computer, looking for the two men. "They should be in the same room, correct? An officer should be with them." Mazey states. Carol finds the information. "Correct Sheriff, they are in room 122 just down the hall. I believe officer Ford is in the room with them." Carol replies. "We are expecting Ranger Evers anytime now, will you send him down to join us?" Mazey asks. Carol responds, "Absolutely sheriff. It was a pleasure to meet you Deputy Weather."

Mazey hurries down the hall. Paul smiles at Carol and quickly follows. The two double time it down the hallway to the room. They see in the distance officer Ford standing outside the room. Coming toward them is an extremely tall man, over seven feet. He is wearing a tank top and dirty jeans, He holds a coat in his hand, his other hand holding a bandage on his shoulder. The three of them make eye contact. The man quickly looks away. Mazey and Paul watch him pass, both feeling a sense of something strange. They make it to room 122. "Ford, glad you're here. Did you get the samples to the lab?" Mazey asks. "Yes, sheriff. They should be ready this afternoon or in the morning." Ford replies. "Did you get statements from the men?" Mazey inquires. "I did, I'll put them in my report when I get back to the office. They are both conscious, but still in a ton of pain." Ford responds. "Good work. Get back to the office, get all the paperwork done and hold the fort. We are waiting for Hocho. We should be back in an hour." Mazey commands. "Yes Ma'am." Ford replies. He tips his cap to Mazey. "Deputy." He addresses Paul and then leaves the area. Mazey and Paul enter the room. Matt White lays in the bed closest to the door. His face is bandaged and bruised. You can see the end of the slashes poking out of the end of the bandage. His head slowly turns as they enter. A long curtain splits the room. Mazey walks over and pushes the curtain open to reveal Al Thorn in the other bed. His torso covered in bandages from where the animal was clawing and gnawing on him. His leg propped up and bandaged from the gunshot. Al opens his eyes as Mazey pushes the curtain fully open to see both men. She looks at Paul. "Will you open those curtains for me?" Paul nods and walks over to the window. He opens the curtain to allow the noon day sun to shine in. The two men wince under the new brightness of the room.

"Sorry to disturb your rest gentlemen, but I have a few questions for you." Mazey begins. "I'll tell you what I told your buddy Joey this morning. I have two men dead way up in the national park. One missing. You two hanging on by a thread. Joey, seemed to have the only sense in the group and ran as fast as he could and jumped in a freezing river." Mazey pauses. She continues. "We need to get to the bottom of this. Did the six of you truly tick off a mama bear deep in those woods, or did you all come to a disagreement and start shooting away?" Mazey looks at both men, who try to adjust their bodies in their beds, hoping the pain will get better. "Al, I'll start with you. Did Bill Molten shoot you? Did you provoke him?" Mazey asks.

Al with as much strength as he can muster responds. "It wasn't a bear. It was a wolf." Mazey stares at him intently. She turns to Paul to see his reaction. Paul looks at the two men's wounds. Mazey addresses Al again. "Was it one wolf, or was there a pack of them?" Matt turns his head and painfully speaks out of the side of his mouth. "It was one wolf. He was tall." Mazey, amazed, moves closer to Matt. "Did you say, He was tall?" She asks. Matt looks at Mazey, she can see the fear still in his eyes. "It stood on its back legs." Matt mutters softly. Mazey looks back at Paul, who suggests. "Sounds like a bear." Al quietly interrupts. "It wasn't a bear; we heard it howl." Mazey inquires again with Matt. "What do you mean He was tall? How tall?" Matt coughs, reeling from the pain. "Over seven feet." He manages to get out. Just then Hocho arrives in the room. Paul and Mazey turn to see him.

"Sheriff. Deputy." Hocho gestures. Mazey turns and walks over to him. "Glad you made it. Did you find the body?" She asks. Hocho, looks at the two gentlemen, who are waiting for his response. "Maybe we should discuss this outside." Hocho states. Mazey, looks back at the two men, knowing the sensitivity. "Get some sleep gentlemen, we will finish this discussion in the morning." Mazey tells Al and Matt. She motions to Paul and Hocho to exit the room. They leave the room and walk down to the end of the hall. "What did you find?" She asks Hocho. "Not much Sheriff. It was Mark Roberts, but his body was pretty picked over. Looked like several animals had their fill throughout the night." Hocho informs. "Jesus, what a mess this is." Mazey replies. "How far off the campsite was he?" Paul asks. Hocho turns to Paul and answers. "I'd say over two miles." Paul turns to Mazey. "What kind of animal can drag a grown man, through the woods that far?" "A large bear. Maybe a mountain lion." Mazey answers. "Are we dealing with multiple animals?" Paul asks. Mazey turns to Hocho. "What else did you see?" she asks. "Sometimes the tracks changed." Hocho answers. "What do you mean changed? Mazey asks. Hocho collects his thought, then answers. "I could see the wolf tracks, and the drag trail of the body. In some spots though, the prints went from four to two."

Paul, curious, asks. "What do you mean? Were they erased? Hocho shakes his head. "There would be a space where the drag track stopped as well." Hocho proclaimed. Mazey, unsure exactly what he was saying, tries to address it. "Are you saying the body was dropped?" Hocho shakes his head again. "No, not dropped. More like it was carried."

Mazey continued to question him. "What about the tracks, where did they go?" Hocho answers. "Not sure, it's like it stood up and walked on hinds legs a bit, then back down." Mazey and Paul looked at each other, both remembering what Al and Matt said. "Does a wolf stand on its hind legs and walk, carry its prey that way? Does a bear?" Paul asks Hocho.

Hocho, thinking, rubs the back of his head and speaks. "I have not seen a wolf stand and carry its prey. I've seen bear stand, but not walk carrying its prey." Mazey ponders what he said. She turns to Paul who awaits her orders. "What do think we are dealing with Ranger?" Mazey asks Hocho. Hocho answers. "Not sure, but whatever it is, has great strength. Was purposeful and had taste for man. I have an uneasy feeling about it. It feels old. Feels evil." The three take a breath, understanding that what they are dealing with may not be solved today or tomorrow.

Mazey breaks the silence. "Good work, Hocho. Go file your report. I'll call you this afternoon if we get the DNA results back. Call me if anything else surfaces." Hocho nods. "Yes, sheriff." He nods to Paul and begins to walk down the hall. Mazey turns to Paul with a small smile on her face. "Good first day so far, huh?" She jokes. Paul manages a small laugh. "Part of the job, isn't it sheriff? Paul returns. Mazey composes herself and manages a small chuckle as well. "He was tall." She states. "Heck of a clue." Paul responds. Mazey starts to walk down the hall. "Time for lunch. I know a great place." She says walking away. Paul smiles and follows after her.

Chapter 6: Pumpkin Pancakes

The downtown square of Forest River Hill is alive and well. The shops and cafés are filled with townsfolk and tourists. The fall decorations adorn the streets and front windows of the local businesses. The large banner that runs over Mainstreet announces their annual Fall Festival scheduled for October 24th through the 30th. Across from the sheriff's office is a town favorite, Bigfoot's Café, home of the famous "Bigfoot and Gravy" dish. Mazey and Paul sit at a booth looking out across from the station. Paul looks over the menu. "What do you usually get?" Paul asks Mazey. She flags a waitress down. "It's been a heck of a morning, so I'm getting the special." She responds. The waitress comes to the table and greets them. "Good morning sheriff, how are you today?"

"Good morning, Becky. Been a day already. Meet my new deputy, Paul Weather." Mazey answers. Becky turns to Paul and greets him. "Welcome, Deputy Weather. So happy you could join us." Paul smiles and responds politely. "It's nice to meet you, Becky." Mazey looks to the other side of the café and spots someone. "Becky, give deputy a minute on the menu, but bring me a hot cup of coffee, a tall unsweet iced tea, and an even taller glass of ice water." Becky writes it down and turns to Paul. "What can I get you to drink?" Paul turns and addresses her. "I'll take a cup of coffee and an ice water, please." Becky writes it down. "Becky is Riley here?" Mazey asks. "I believe she is. Do you want me to go ask her to come over?" Becky responds. "If you don't mind." Mazey confirms. "Let me get your drinks, and I'll tell Riley to come over and visit." Becky informs then leaves the table.

Paul continues to scan the menu. Mazey opens the roll of silverware, placing the fork and knife on her left side and the napkin in her lap. She then reaches over and grabs four packs of sugar and three creamers from the condiment tray on the table. She peers down the café to see Riley walking toward them. Riley is a tall, attractive lady, with long wavy dark brown hair. She is dressed professionally and walks with confidence. She is well known and smiles at many of the other patrons on her way to their table. She arrives at the table and greets Mazey. "Well good morning, Sheriff Keller. How are you today?" Paul turns and notices her. "Thanks for coming over, Riley. I wanted to introduce our new deputy. This is Paul Weather. Paul, this is Riley Forest. She is one hell of a Criminal Defense Attorney here in town. Her family also owns this restaurant, and several places here in town." Paul smiles and extends his hand to her. "It's a pleasure to meet you counselor." Riley shakes his hand and smiles in return. "Happy to meet you, deputy. Welcome to Forest River Hill, and especially to Bigfoot Café." The two exchange a nice glance at each other, the attraction is immediate. Mazey notices.

"Riley and I went to high school together. We both played softball and ran cross country." Mazey explains. "Yes, and now we get into heated debates from time to time about our criminal justice system." Riley retorts. "Exactly, Riley believes in the old adage, innocent until proven guilty. While I believe in the old saying 'trust your gut'." Mazey adds. "We still make a good team though." Riley adds. She turns to Paul, whose gaze is still upon her. "Deputy are you from around here?" She asks. "No, not originally. I was born and raised in Florida. But I am very fond of the pacific northwest." Paul responds. "Florida, fantastic. My sister has a place right on the water in Cocoa Beach." Riley states. "I spent my childhood right next door in a town called Merritt Island. Just south of the Kennedy Space Center." Paul replies.

A quick pause as the two admire each other. Mazey interrupts. "Can you suggest something for Paul's first meal here in our special little town?" Paul, excited, waits to hear Riley's answer. "Well now that fall is arriving the best dish on the menu this time of year is Bigfoot Café's homemade Pumpkin Pancakes. We make them out of fresh pumpkins from our own patch, then mix in graham cracker crust into the batter, cinnamon, and a dash of cloves. Topped with fresh whip cream and our hot pecan maple syrup." Paul already starving is greatly intrigued. "I believe you sold me." He states. Riley smiles. "When Becky comes back, tell her that is what you want, and tell her you want it the Riley way." She adds. Paul, intrigued, asks her what that includes. "The Riley way? What does that include" "That includes four slices of our applewood smoked bacon, and a cup of fresh fruit." Riley responds.

Paul looks at Mazey, she is amused by the interaction between the two of them. "You are going to want it the Riley Way." She says. Paul turns back to Riley. "That is what I'm getting then. Pumpkin Pancakes, the Riley way. Thank you for suggesting." Riley smiles at Paul. "You are welcome!" Riley responds. She turns to Mazey. "I am in a lunch meeting still, so I need to return. But I'll call you this afternoon. I heard about the incident in the national park." She turns back to Paul. "It was a pleasure meeting you, deputy. I'm sure we'll be working together soon." Riley states. "It was great to meet you. Looking forward to the pancakes." Paul responds. "Have a great lunch, I'll speak with you later." Riley speaks and leaves the table. Mazey gives Paul a look, as if he almost misbehaved.

"First day and you already have a case and a new friend." Mazey jokes. "You've known her since high school?" Paul asks. Becky returns to the table and puts down their drinks. "Longer than that, our families have lived in this town close to four generations now." Mazey responds. Becky grabs her pen and pad. "What can I get you two to eat?" she asks. "I want the usual, Bigfoot and Gravy. Throw on top of that, three eggs scrambled and a side of grits." Mazey requests. "Yes ma'am. And what can I get for you, deputy?" Becky asks. "I have been advised to order the Pumpkin Pancakes." Paul states. "Excellent choice, they're my favorite this time of year. Anything else to go with them?" Becky asks. Paul smiles and responds. "I have also been advised to have them the Riley way." Mazey sips her coffee and shakes her head. "Excellent. I will get this order in, check back in a few minutes with some coffee refills." Becky states. "Thanks Becky!" Mazey replies. Becky smiles and walks away.

Paul, intrigued, finally asks. "So, what the heck is 'Bigfoot and Gravy'?" Mazey, with a quirky laugh, responds. "As you know, we are in 'bigfoot' country. Riley's dad, who ran this place the last forty years, during the days when we used to have a ton of sightings, decided to make a special to attract the tourists. It is basically a huge plate of biscuits topped with homemade sausage gravy. He had the local blacksmith make him a cookie cutter in the shape of a bigfoot imprint. So basically, you get a large plate, with a large biscuit shaped like a big foot, topped with homemade goodness."

Paul shakes his head. "That makes total sense. Next time I'm all over that, unless these Pumkin Pancakes are all they are cracked up to be." He states. "Let's enjoy the meal, we still have a lot to cover this afternoon. Hopefully, the DNA results will be ready, and we can make some headway on what the hell happened up in the woods." Mazey says. The two both enjoy their coffee and the atmosphere of the restaurant.

Chapter 7: A Naked Bigfoot

Back at the station Paul is at his new deputy desk. He is enduring the slow but necessary process of filing his report, including getting all his systems set up for him to access. He belches quietly, a result of the filling pumpkin pancakes he enjoyed at the café. Mazey walks around the corner from her office, a file in her hand. She heads straight for Paul's desk. "Paul, put a halt on the onboarding for a second and come talk to the witness from this morning with me." She states. "Roger, that." He responds thankfully. Paul grabs a pen and pad and follows Mazey back to her office.

Inside, sitting in one of the chairs is Alice Higgins, who viewed and reported the naked man in her yard this morning. Mazey walks around and sits at her desk, Paul stands off to the side. "Sorry, Alice I wanted my new deputy to hear your report. This is Deputy Paul Weather; he joined us today." Mazey states. "It is a pleasure to meet you, deputy" Alice politely greets. "The pleasure is all mine, ma'am." Paul responds. "Alice, please if you will, tell the deputy what you told me about what you saw in the yard this morning." Mazey requests. Alice nods her head and turns slightly to Paul to address him. "Certainly. I was out in my back porch, which I am almost every morning, weather permitted. I was drinking my coffee and reading a book. I also do a little bird watching. We have some great birds in the national forest. While I was reading, I heard what sounding like moaning, as if someone was in pain. My eyes are not what they used to be, but I had my binoculars on the table, so I reached for them. Well, I couldn't believe what I saw. It was a grown man, naked as the day he was born, laying in my field. I dropped the binoculars, hoping it was an illusion. The man stood up. So, I peered at him one more time. He was covered in grass and mud. He looked in my direction, which startled me. I may have said something, and then suddenly he ran off. He jumped the fence like a gazelle and disappeared." Mazey looks over at Paul who is writing some of this down.

Mazey interjects. "Can you describe what the man looked like?" Alice readjusts herself in the chair and turns back to Mazey to respond. "Well, I don't know, it happened so fast. I know I saw him through binoculars, but he appeared to be really tall. Even when I dropped the binoculars and saw him run away, he looked big from a distance." Paul drops the pen and addresses Alice. "Were there any markings or features on him that you could identify or recognize?" Alice ponders for a moment. "It is all a blur now. He had dark, dark black hair I remember. He kind of looked like that quiet gentleman that owns the woodshop on the edge of town. He ran so fast; it was hard to get a good look. He was covered in grass and mud, his stride was long, he looked like a naked bigfoot running away." Alice finishes. Mazey hides her small laugh as to how Alice describes the man.

"Do you think you could point him out of a line-up of men if we can gather some suspects?" Mazey asks. "I don't know. If they were all naked, maybe." Alice smiles. Paul now tries to hide his laughter. "Did you get the arm, sheriff? Maybe you can find out whose arm it was?" Alice asks. Mazey responds. "Yes, we have that in evidence down at the lab now. We should know something by tomorrow." Mazey closes the file in front of her. "Thank you so much Alice for coming down to the station. Let us know if you see anything else, or if something comes back to your memory about the naked man."

"This has been really scary, especially since I lost Carl in the spring. My daughter usually comes by, but her and the family are away. Is there any way you can send an officer by sometime after sunset, just to check on me and walk my yard?" Alice asks in earnest. Mazey responds in kind. "Absolutely, I will send Officer Jackson by tonight when he comes on shift. He will search your whole property, make sure all your doors and windows are safe. Will that be, okay?" Alice stands to her feet. "That would be great. Let officer Jackson know I'll have some dinner for him if he is hungry." Mazey stands. Alice extends her hand to the sheriff. Mazey shakes and gives her a comforting smile. Alice turns to Paul and extends her hand as well. "Welcome to Forest River Hill, deputy." She says politely. Paul kindly shakes her hand and smiles. "We will find this tall man for you. Don't worry." He assures her. Alice smiles and walks out of the office. Mazey sits back down. Paul walks over and sits in a chair in front of her desk.

"A naked tall man, and an arm? What are we looking at?" Paul asks. Mazey responds. "Not sure yet. Could be connected to our guys in the woods. Could be a whole separate incident. We will know more when the labs come back." Paul looks at the notes he took. "Who is this man she mentioned who owns a woodshop? Are you familiar with him?" He asks. "I know about the man and shop, but I have never met him. I do know from other people in town who have ordered items from him that he is quiet. We can run by tomorrow and check the place out. The labs should shine a better light on what or who did this." Mazey responds.

"Alice seemed like a nice lady. What a thing to experience first thing in the morning. She must have been terrified." Paul states. Mazey smiles and responds. "Don't let her fool you. Alice Higgins is a stubborn, tough ole bird. She is also the town's queen gossiper. She makes a point to be in everyone's business. Her husband Carl ran the town newspaper for forty years. She will tell you she knows everyone in town, and she may well be right." Mazey pulls open a drawer in her desk and grabs a set of keys. She tosses the set on the desk in front of Paul. "Need to give you those today. That set is the doors, the jails, ammo cabinets, and I believe the set to your cruiser, which is out back. It's like mine, just not a 250, but a 150. Still a 4x4 though. One day, when I retire, somebody will get the big truck." She smiles but isn't joking.

Paul grabs the keys and looks them over. "Go and finish your onboarding, I think we have done all we can today. We should have received the labs by now, so we probably won't get them until the morning." Mazey states. "Sounds good. I need to finish my report as well." Paul responds. Mazey looks at her watch. "Go ahead and head out when you're done, I'm sure you need to unpack and get settled. Is there anything you need help with?" She asks. Paul ponders, thinking back on the day so far. "Where is the best place to grab some groceries. I will need some coffee and water for sure, maybe some quick things I can whip up in the kitchen, toiletries, etc." Paul asks.

Mazey opens her drawer again and finds a small tourist map of the town. She hands it over to Paul. "There is a grocery store three blocks off the square, heading toward your house on State Road 32. They should have everything you need." Paul grabs the map from her. "Perfect. I also noticed that there were no televisions in the house. Is there a good bookstore in town where I can swing by and get some reading material? He asks. Mazey smiles, realizing the house is a tad rustic. "Yes, sorry. The house does have Wi-Fi, but the last person that lived there removed all the televisions. You remember where the café was across the street?" she asks. Paul pats his belly. "How could I forget." He states. "Okay, go south down that block and turn right, you will see a shop called 'Nadia's Books, Gifts & Lore.' Nadia is kind of the town historian. She can be a little creepy, but her head is full of a million facts. She will find you exactly what you need." Mazey explains. Paul smiles, grabs the map, and keys and stands up. "Sounds great, thanks. I'll go finish up. I'll come see you when I'm done."

"Great work today. Sorry you got thrown right into it, but I'm glad you're here." Mazey states. Paul smiles in appreciation. "For God and Country, right?" He says. Mazey acknowledges the soldier in him. "For God and Country!" she responds back. Paul turns and heads to leave the office. "Please close the door behind you, I have to make some calls." Mazey requests. Paul follows orders and closes the door as he leaves.

Mazey picks up her cell phone and makes a call. The phone rings twice and then a woman answers on the other line. "Hello." "Hey, Solia. You have the kids?" Mazey asks. Solia responds. "Yes, Ma'am." "Okay, great. Make sure they start their homework. If you can make that chicken casserole tonight that would be great. I should be there in about two hours." Mazey informs. "Will do." Solia confirms. "Okay, I will see you around six." Mazey states and hangs up. She puts the phone down and leans back in her chair. She takes a deep breath and rubs her eyes. She looks out the window, the shadows changing, and the sun starting its descent behind the mountains. She looks at the door, making sure it is closed. She opens the bottom file drawer on her left. It opens revealing a few bottles of liquor. She pulls out a half full big bottle of Jack Daniels. She grabs a coffee cup on her desk and looks inside. Just a swallow left of cold black coffee from this morning.

She chokes down the last bit of cold coffee from the cup. "Ugh, gross." She responds to the taste. She opens the Jack Daniels and pours a few ounces into the cup. She takes a good sip and leans back into her chair. "Ahh, much better." As she thinks about the day, small laughs leap out of her. She takes another sip. Another deep breath. "A naked bigfoot!" Another small laugh at the thought of that phrase. "Perfect." She proclaims. She drinks the rest of the cup.

Chapter 8: Lyconology

The sun is starting its descent behind the mountains, a good hour and a half of sunlight still remains. That light shines on the front window of 'Nadia's Books, Gifts & Lore.' Paul walks inside. The side walls are covered with shelves of gifts, trinkets, and a few souvenirs related to the town. A small checkout counter in the middle of the shop. Paul notices paintings around the shop that appear to be centuries old and depict old battles, castles, and beasts of all kinds. A circle staircase leads up to a second floor and next to the staircase is a black curtain that hides another room. There is a soft Celtic music playing over the speakers, and candles and incense create an inviting aroma to the place. Paul peers around but does not see any books. Suddenly the curtain opens, and a tall striking woman comes though. Shiney, straight dark hair. Strong facial feature with piercing blue-grey eyes. Her stride is smooth, her black boots almost completely covered by a shimmering silver long dress.

"Good afternoon, sorry for the wait, I was moving some books around in the back." Nadia explains, in her European accent. "You must be our new deputy." She states. Paul, surprised she knew who he was, then quickly realized he still had his uniform on. "Yes. I'm off duty, so just doing a little shopping." Nadia walks up close to him. She extends her hand. "I am Nadia Vlademia, owner of this small shop." Paul shakes her hand. "Pleasure to meet you Nadia, I am Paul Weather." Nadia looks at his hand, she turns it from side to side. "You are from the east coast, a beach town perhaps?" Nadia suggests. Paul smiles, unsure how she knew that. "Your freckles are beautiful, a design of years in the sun. Your shade as well. Nobody here in the pacific northwest gets that opportunity." She states. "You're good. Born and raised in Florida, the sunshine state." Paul responds.

"Are you here for a souvenir, or can I interest you in something more important?" Nadia asks. Paul looks around. "I was hoping you had some books. They have me at a house in the woods, so I wanted to take advantage of the quiet and catch up on my reading." Nadia smiles. "I'm sure we can find something that would interest you. Follow me, deputy." Nadia turns and walks back to the black curtain and opens it. She nods for him to follow. Paul walks to her and beyond the curtain. He enters a good-sized room, filled with shelves and bookcases covered in books. All kinds. Paperback, hard cover, old books, new titles, and many in shapes and designs he is unfamiliar with. There is a large glass case against the back wall that houses what looked like old style weapons from times long ago.

"What kind of books do you normally read?" Nadia asks. Paul continues to look around at all the different, odd things in the room. "Nothing too serious, just entertaining. I normally read a good mystery, historical fiction, or an entertaining creature feature novel." Paul states. "Well, we have all of those, so please look around. I will be out front if you need me." Nadia states, she smiles and walks back to the front of the store. Paul walks around each bookcase. His eyes, searching for a title, or an author that is familiar. He makes his way back to the glass case with all the old weapons. Several knives which shape and design he has never seen. A few guns, which look straight out of world war one, with shiny bullets next to them. To his right he sees a tall bookshelf filled with large black books, foreign words written on them in several different languages.

Out front Nadia stands at the checkout counter. She looks on the floor where Paul came through and sees a few hairs glistening in the afternoon sun and reflecting off the glass. She walks around and picks them up. She holds them into the light. The hair almost reflects as if it has silver or glass in it. She walks back around the corner and puts them on the counter. She turns around to a dresser behind her and opens the top drawer. She pulls out what looks like a small metal microscope. She grabs a piece of the hair and puts it on the plate. She turns the microscope light on and looks through the lens. She is startled. She pulls away from the viewfinder. Slowly she returns and looks again. The black curtain opens, and Paul reappears into the front room carrying books. Nadia turns away from the microscope and stands at the counter waiting. "Found something, did you?" She asks. Paul smiles as he comes around to the counter and puts two books down. "I did, thank you. Great collection by the way. What is with all those old knives and guns, are they for sale? Paul asks. Nadia smiles and grabs the books. She enters them into the computer. "Thank you. No, those are not for sale. Those are for story time. A collection of trinkets passed along many generations of my family. The word 'Lore' in our name, is what we call our stories we tell the children on the weekend."

Paul reaches into his pocket and pulls out his wallet. The hair from the crime scene comes out and lands on the counter. Nadia grabs a bag for the books and notices the hair fall. It appears similar to the other hairs she found on the ground. She puts the books in the bag. She grabs the hair off of the counter. "Where did this come from?" She asks. "Oh, sorry, that was from a crime scene this morning." Paul responds. "Do you mind if I look at it closer?" Nadia asks. Paul was unsure why she would want to. "Sure, knock yourself out." He replies. Nadia turns again and places the hair on the microscope. She looks at all the hairs together. They are the same. They all shine, as if they have tiny silver or diamonds woven into them. Nadia hands the hair back to Paul. "Do you know what animal this is?" She asks. Paul cautiously takes the hair and puts it back in his pocket. "We are not sure yet. Could be a bear. Could be a wolf." Paul opens his wallet. "How much for the books?" He asks, wanting to hurry up and leave.

Nadia stares into his eyes. "Do you mind, just for a second. I have a book for you." She states. Paul, curious now. "Sure." He replies. Nadia walks to the back room. Paul picks up the hair from the counter, he examines it closely. Putting it back in his pocket he peers over to the microscope, noticing how old it looks. The light is different, not a typical shade of a lightbulb, but cleaner, softer. He sees a sign above the microscope that reads, 'Fiction is just non-fiction, sprinkled with imagination.'

Nadia returns from the back with a large black book. The spine has a word written in a foreign language. The cover has engraved into it the head of a wolf. "Sorry about that, I remembered a book you may enjoy, since you said creature feature." She says, placing the book inside the bag with the others. Paul curiously asks. "What is that book about?" Nadia ponders a second. "Have you ever read Bram Stokers *Dracula*?" She asks. "A long time ago." Paul responds. "It is similar to that. Several stories of journeys and encounters, but instead of a vampire, it revolves around the legend of the werewolf. It goes over the folklore, the origin stories, and the history of its evolution. Some refer to it as a

Book of Lyconology, or the study of werewolves. I know you will find it interesting." She states.

Paul reaches for a card in his wallet. "Thank you, I'll definitely check it out. Now, how much do I owe you?" He asks. Nadia politely responds. "Please consider this a welcome gift. We are thankful you have come to help Sheriff Keller. These books are my present to you." Paul smiles. He puts the card back in the wallet and the wallet back in his pocket. "That is very kind of you. I promise to read a lot while I am here, so I shall return to purchase more books." Paul grabs the bag from the counter. "You have been so helpful. It has been a pleasure to meet you, Nadia. The light is fading, and I still have to go to the grocery store and drive to the house. I'd like to make it before dark." Paul kindly states. Nadia smiles, she reaches out to shake his hand. Paul obliges and shakes her hand. "It is great to meet you as well, deputy. I look forward to seeing you around town. If you need anything else, please do not hesitate to come and see me. I know a great deal about this town and will be a useful place of information for you." Nadia exclaims. Paul smiles and releases the handshake. "You have a good evening." Paul says kindly as he turns and walks out of the store. Nadia watches him leave and head down the street. She grabs a small box next to the microscope. She puts the hairs in the box. She turns off the microscope and places it back in the drawer.

She takes the box and walks back behind the curtain to the back room, then heads to the tall bookcase, next to the glass case with the old items. Nadia grabs a book from the shelf and opens it. Inside the book is a large metal key. She removes the key and places the book down. She uses the key to unlock the glass case. She places the small box with the hairs into the glass case and closes it up. She places the key back in the book, and the book back on the bookcase. Nadia takes a deep breath, then quietly says, "The moon shines, as the hunter arrives."

Chapter 9: Nightfall

The orange, blue, and purple hues paint the sunset as Mazey pulls up to her house nestled down a tree lined road. The lights are on, and Solia and the kids can be seen around the dining area and kitchen. Mazey exits the vehicle and walks up the front porch and into the house. The smell of food hits her, and the warmth of her own house allows her to take a deep breath and drop the cares of the day. "It smells delicious, Solia!" Mazey announces her presence. She walks across the front room and into the dining room where her children sit. "Hey, mommy!" Her ten-year-old son, Corey responds first. He sits at the table, drawing something in a book as he awaits dinner. "Hi, mom." The older child, the thirteen-year-old daughter, Katie, chimes in as well. Mazey walks in and kisses them both on the forehead. Solia comes out of the kitchen with food in hand and brings it to the table. "Just in time Ms. Mazey. Everything is ready." Solia announces.

Mazey turns to notice another girl at the table. "Mom is it okay that Lia has dinner with us? We were working on some homework together. Mrs. Anderson said she will be here by 8:00 pm to pick her up." Katie states. Mazey turns to look at Lia, a sweet slender girl, Katie's age, kind eyes and a keen mind. "Absolutely, I'm sure we have plenty of food, and I'm glad to hear you are getting homework done. Happy to see you, Lia." Mazey says. "Thank you, Sheriff Keller." Lia responds softly. "You are welcome, honey. Please call me Ms. Mazey, you aren't in trouble so the Sheriff, doesn't have to be used." Mazey explains. Lia confirms. "Yes, Ms. Mazey."

Mazey takes off her gun belt and places it on a side table, she sits down between her two kids. Solia finishes bringing everyone's plates to them. Solia sits down when she finishes. "This looks incredible, Solia. Thank you! Corey, will you say grace?" Mazey asks. Corey closes his drawing book and puts down his pencil. He folds his hands and closes his eyes. Everyone else at the table follows as well. "Thank you, God, for bringing my mommy home safely today. Please protect her on her job. Thank you for this meal. Thank you for our friend, Lia. Thank you for Solia. Bless this food for our body. Amen." The others agree by saying 'Amen.'

They grab their forks and begin to eat. "Thank you, little man, that was perfect. Katie, what are you and Lia working on?" Mazey asks. Katie finishing swallowing her bite of food. "It is a project for science class. It is on different types of animal species. Lia and I are writing it on the history of wolves." Katie states. Mazey, a tad surprised considering the day. "Wolves? That is interesting. Should have good information in this part of the world. Our national park system houses many breeds of wolves." Mazey responds. Katie chews another bite of food, washes it down with her iced tea. "Lia and I have been watching some videos about all the different types. Many surviving in the pacific northwest. Didn't realize there were so many different ones." Katie says. Mazey, enjoying the casserole she suggested Solia make, finishes her bite. "Hard to believe they were close to being extinct around here. The parks became a sanctuary for them and allowed them to rebuild their numbers. Allowed us to study them, identify their kinds." Mazey states.

"Yes, Lia and I have to write on the three types of wolves we like the best for our homework." Katie states. "Lia, which wolf is your favorite?" Mazey asks, to get her involved in the conversation. Lia finishes the food in her mouth and puts down her fork. "The one I like;

we could not find a video for." She softly responds. Mazey curious.

"Which wolf is that?" She asks. "My grandfather told me a story of a great wolf, which hides deep in the woods. He said it is bigger and faster than all wolves. He called it a Wechuge." Mazey is now even more curious. "Did your grandfather ever see one?" Mazey asks. "He told a story about when he was camping just across the border in Canada. It attacked some horses at a ranch he was staying at. My grandfather said he shot it four times. As he went to go see if it was dead, he said it stood up, like a bear on two legs, then ran deep into the woods. That night he could hear it howl in the distance."

Mazey sits back in her chair. Taking in the story Lia is telling. Katie smiles, as if she believes Lia is pulling her mom's leg. "Well, that sounds more like a campfire legend than the actual wolves we have around here. If we had some actual video footage or books about it, we could include it. We need to cite all of our resources, and grandparents aren't on the education protocol list." Katie interjects.

Mazey keeps her focus on Lia, her face shows that she is telling the truth. "Well, good thing. Sounds like you would not want to come face to face with an animal like that. Good thing your grandfather was not hurt." Mazey responds to Lia. "He has never seen the wolf again, but he does tell me that from time to time, late at night, he will hear its howl." Lia says as she looks deeply at Mazey. Everyone pauses for a moment, no chewing, no speaking, just a silence at the table.

The silence is interrupted by the doorbell. Everyone is startled out of their silence. "Oh, for heaven's sake. At this time of night." Solia states and starts to get up to answer it. "No, Solia, I'll get it. Probably Lia's mom here early to pick her up." Mazey interrupts. Mazey gets up, Solia sits back down. She grabs her gun belt from the table and puts it back on. Lia looks toward the door, and then to Mazey. "It is Mayor Moorehouse." Lia states plainly. Mazey looks at her, not sure how she would know that. Mazey makes her way out of the dining room, across the front room and to the door. She opens it. Standing on the porch is a well-dressed man, slightly overweight, well-groomed salt and pepper hair and beard. He stands with a concerned look on his face. Mazey, a bit shocked. "Mayor Moorehouse! What can I do for you?"

The Mayor motions for her to come out onto the porch. Mazey steps out and closes the door behind her. "Sorry for interrupting your dinner, but I need to tell you something so you can prepare." The Mayor informs. "What is it?" Mazey asks. "I got a call from the military base today. You know they own about one-hundred thousand acres of the park." He states. "I do. What did they want?" Mazey asks. "Apparently Ranger Evers, crossed their fence line on his tracking this morning. He was gone before they could find him, but they did recover the body." Moorhouse states. "Jesus, are they keeping it, or letting us, have it? It is our investigation." Mazey replies. "I am sure we will get it back. They are more pissed Hocho trespassed on their side. Please make sure he understands what boundaries he can and cannot cross." The mayor, frustrated, rubbed his beard to calm himself. "Anyway, I wanted you to know there will be an officer at your office tomorrow morning to discuss the incident. We all know they are doing some crazy stuff up there in the hills, but we keep away, and we don't ask questions. This town gets a fat-ass check from the government to keep a lid on this base, and I intend to keep it that way." The mayor states.

Mazey adjusts her gun belt, as she is now frustrated as well. "I'll speak to Hocho. I'm sure he had a great reason to go into the area, but I will address it with him. Are you hungry, do you want to come in for some food?" Mazey asks. "I am hungry, but we have a stupid meeting about the fall festival. I'm sure we have food catered in. The meeting will be boring and long, I'm sure. Just have your story straight tomorrow for the military and keep your people away from their fence." The mayor responds. "You got it, sir. Say hi to the council for me. Find out how many of my staff will be needed for the festival and if I need to get a volunteer staff for it." Mazey asks. "I will, now get back to dinner, sorry to interrupt." The mayor responds and quickly walks off the porch, into his car and drives away. Mazey watches as he leaves. She heads back inside the house.

Walking back into the dining room, she sits down. "So, it wasn't Lia's mom?" Katie asks. Mazey looks over at Lia. "No, it wasn't her mom." Lia eats her dinner, happy and content. "Lia, how did you know it was the mayor?" She asks. "It was the mayor! Holy crap, Lia, good guess." Katie, happy and excited, cheers on Lia. Lia finishes the bite in her mouth as Mazey awaits her response. Mazey asks again. "How did you know it was the mayor?" Lia puts down her fork, thinking. She then turns to Mazey. "I don't know. I just saw him in my mind right before the doorbell rang." Mazey sits back in her chair. "You saw him in your mind?" She asks. "Like a picture. Then he was here." Mazey ponders what she says. "What did he want?" Katie asks. Mazey leans forward and picks up her fork. "It was nothing. Just about the fall festival. Everyone, finish eating. When you are done Katie, you and Lia go to your room and finish the homework. Corey, honey, you, and I can hit the couch and watch a movie. How does that sound?" Mazey asks. Corey, still with some food in his mouth. "Can we watch Thor?" He muddles. Mazey smiles and nods. "Yes, for the one hundredth time, we can watch Thor." The girls shake their head, knowing that is his favorite movie at this time. They finish the dinner, conversing and laughing.

Meanwhile, across town, Paul is busy in the kitchen putting away the groceries he bought at the store. Sprawled out across the counter are the necessities of water, coffee, snacks, toiletries, some bottles of wine and beer, and frozen dinners. He is trying to start a system of where everything should go and how he will remember it. As he is putting a stack of napkins on the dining room table, he notices the shed next to the river. The lights are on inside of it. He doesn't think much of it. He checks his phone to see the time. He put a few more groceries away. Paul grabs a bottle of wine and starts to open it. He turns toward the window as he opens the wine, and this time he sees what appears to be a shadow moving inside the shed. Pausing the opening of the wine, he moves closer to the window. Again, what appears to be a figure, dark, moving inside the shed. Paul puts the wine bottle down. He walks to the kitchen counter where he had put his utility belt from his uniform. Paul grabs his issued gun, flashlight, and the keys to the shed.

The sounds of the forest fill his ears as he walks out of the house, down the back porch and begins what seems a hundred-yard trek to the shed. He imagines in his mind it may be a squatter. Maybe someone realizing the house is empty and has taken cover from the elements inside the shed. As Paul quickly makes his way to the shed, he raises his gun in front of him, along with flashlight, not sure if there is someone inside, or whether they are armed or not. Suddenly a howl comes from deep inside the forest. It startles Paul. He stops in his track. He looks and points the gun in each direction, making sure nothing is near him or behind him. Secured, Paul carries on toward the shed. "Hello!" Paul shouts as he gets closer, hoping he hears a response and can confirm someone's presence.

Paul stops just a few feet away from the shed door. Aiming the gun dead center on the door he speaks again. "This is Deputy Weather, I am armed. Is someone inside the shed?" Paul waits. He listens for movement or a sound. Nothing. Just the rhythm of the stream next to him and the song of the insects in the forest. He notices the lock is secured on the door. If someone is in there, they are locked in. Paul slowly grabs the key to unlock the door. "I am unlocking the door and opening it. Once again, I am Deputy Weather, and my gun is drawn. Please put down any weapon you may have." Paul unlocks and removes the lock. He slowly grabs the handle on the door. Takes a deep breath and aims his gun. Quickly he opens the door. Buzzing by his head is a large Owl or Hawk from inside the shed. "Jesus!" Paul shrieks as the bird startles him. He almost squeezes out a round, but at the last minute realizes it is some sort of bird.

Paul collects himself and lowers his gun. He peers inside the shed. No person inside. He makes his way in. On the floor are a couple carcasses of mice. Obviously, food for whatever bird was trapped inside. Paul's breathing slows down. He composes himself and investigates the shed. Inside the shed is a mix of lawn equipment, tools, bags of soil, fertilizer, and pebbles. On the back wall is a row of axes, shovels, pitchforks, and other bladed tools for gardening. A long bench across one of the sides that has electric tools, animal traps and rolls of rope, chain, and fence material. On the other wall is a locked gun cabinet filled with handguns, rifles, shotguns and accompanied ammunition. Paul looks around and around, searching for any sign of human life. Nothing. It appears the shadow he saw was the bird. "I need some sleep." Paul says out loud to himself.

He turns to leave the shed. Seeing the light switch on the wall next to the door he turns out the lights. He closes the door and puts the lock back on and locks it. Paul puts the keys away in his pocket and turns toward the stream. The water shimmers with the moonlight slowly rising. The sound of the water moving is soothing to his ears. Remembering he was opening the bottle of wine before the shadow startled him, he smiles. "Where was I? Oh, yes Paul, you were about to pour yourself a glass of wine?" He says out loud. Paul turns and begins the trek back to the house. Ten paces away, another loud howl. Paul quickly turns and raises the gun. He looks intently passed the shed. Passed the stream, into the darkness of the forest, something is moving. His eyes adjust, locked in on anything that moves.

There they were. Two eyes. Glowing through the thickness of the forest and the night. Paul steadies his aim, fixed on whatever is watching him. The eyes are steady. Paul's aim is steady. Neither is budging. Paul raises the gun slowly toward the sky. He pulls the trigger. The shot clangs through the night air. It worked, the eyes turned and disappeared into the forest. Paul waits a beat, now feeling that he is safe, he lowers his gun, turns toward the house, and walks back.

Chapter 10: Military Involvement

Mazey sips her coffee at her desk. The sun is just starting to shine. The frost clinging to the window, a bit early, but not unheard of up at this elevation. Her mind is filled of thoughts, from the military man coming this morning, to the dead bodies, awaiting the DNA, Hocho stepping across the fence line, and how her new deputy will adjust. With all that weighing her down, Mazey reaches into the bottom drawer again, grabs a bottle and pours a tiny shot of liquor in her coffee cup.

May taps on her door. She sips her coffee and puts it down. "Come in." she projects. May opens the door and walks to her desk, she hands her a folder. "Little cold this morning, don't you think?" May asks. "Colder than normal, maybe." Mazey responds. "The Military gentleman is here. I offered coffee, but he refused. He is sitting down waiting." May remarks. "Give me a few more minutes, then send him in. Is Deputy Weather here yet?" Mazey asks. "I believe I just saw him pull up. "Would you like me to send him in?" May asks. "Let him get a coffee if he doesn't have one and send him in." Mazey states. "Will do. By the way, I know your busy, but we had a message on the phone last night, and an actual call this morning of more people claiming they saw someone running naked through their yard." May says.

Mazey looks at her, hoping she was joking and asks. "Did they say when this happened?" "The one that called last night, called just after ten pm and said they saw it. The one this morning said they saw someone just before dawn running out of their barn." May answered. Mazey sat back in her chair, not sure if these are real statements or just townsfolks seeing things. "Call them back and see if they will come in and give a statement on record. Call Hocho, see if he can get here as soon as he can. Send Deputy Weather in, then the military representative." Mazey states. "You got it, boss." May responds. She smiles and heads back out of the office, shutting the door.

Mazey stands and heads to her window overlooking the downtown square. She sees the military vehicle parked outside her office. "Take your bumps and smile, Mazey. Don't make waves." She says to herself. A knock at her door. "Come in." She responds. The door opens and Paul walks in, coffee in hand, uniform clean and ironed, fully equipped and ready to serve. "Good morning, Sheriff." Paul greets her. She walks back from the window and sits at her desk. "Did you sleep well?" She asks. Paul walks over to the desk. "Surprisingly yes. Must have been those few days on the road getting here. I'm sure my body was tired." He responds.

"Good. Do me a favor, greet the man coming in, sit down, then be quiet unless I ask you a question. I'll explain this madness when we are done." Mazey states. Paul quietly responds, "Yes Ma'am." The door opens and May enters with the military man behind her in full dress uniform. "Sheriff. Deputy. This is Colonel Marcus Riser" May announces. Colonel Riser walks over and shakes Mazey's hand. "Sheriff." He greets. "Colonel, glad you could be here this morning. This is my Deputy, Paul Weather." Mazey states. Paul shakes the Colonel's hand and greets him, "Good morning, Colonel." "Deputy Weather." The Colonel responds. "Pleas, have a seat." Mazey requests. Paul and Colonel Riser sit down. Mazey does as well.

"What can we do for you, Colonel?" Mazey asks. The Colonel pauses for a moment and collects his thought. "I'll make this brief. There was an unauthorized civilian within our base walls yesterday. Forest Ranger Hocho Evers. He was seen on our surveillance cameras, but exited the perimeter, before we could apprehend him. The body he evidently was looking for, we have already collected and are doing our own research on. We will transport the body to you sometime this evening or tomorrow morning when our examination is complete." The Colonel states.

Paul was in a little shock finding out there is a military base in the national park that is not listed on public record. "Hocho was on order from me to locate the body, we were unaware it was within the base perimeters. It is part of a murder scene in the park that we are investigating." Mazey explains. "General Ford has informed me that we will not be arresting Ranger Evers this time. However, He also informed me that any further trespassing on the base will be considered an act of trespassing on government property. If one of your officers is found within the base or any park rangers, they will be apprehended on site and charged with crimes against the United States. Are we clear on these requests?" The Colonel stated emphatically. Mazey, trying not to show how angry she was, takes a deep breath and calms herself.

"We understand completely, Colonel. I will address my team this morning and speak to Ranger Evers as well. It will not happen again." Mazey responds. "I know the Mayor reminded you of how well the base funds this town. Any violation of our request will result in the removal of those funds. Remember Sheriff, we are an asset to you. We have been clear for several decades now that we will respond to any emergency this town has, and if you ever need additional forces for any reason, our base will supply them. Just keep off our base! We both know your family has been safeguarding this town for generations. There has been no military involvement into your office or your authority. I know you do not wish to have any in the future." The Colonel concludes.

Paul watches Mazey. He sees the frustration in her eyes but admires her calm and resolve in this situation. Mazey stands up. "Thank you, Colonel, for addressing this with us this morning. I will advise my team. Please thank the General for his kindness towards Ranger Evers. I know he will be grateful." The Colonel stands. He stares intently at Mazey. The two shake hands. "The morgue will contact you when we deliver the body." The Colonel turns to Paul, who stands and shakes his hand as well. "Nice to meet you, Deputy." The Colonel states.

"Likewise, Colonel." Paul responds. The Colonel turns and walks out of the office. Mazey follows and shuts the door behind him. She takes a deep breath and blows out her frustration.

"What in the hell was that?" Paul asks. Mazey walks back to her desk and refills her coffee cup from the pot behind her desk. She sits back down and takes a sip from her mug. "Last time I checked, there is no public knowledge of a military base in this area." Paul states. Mazey looks at him and smirks. "Unfortunately, you are on a need-to-know basis, and right now the only thing you need to know is there is a military facility in the National Park, and it is strictly off limits to non-military." Mazey states. "What the hell are they doing up there?" Paul asks. "The last three Sheriff's that have sat in this chair have tried to figure that out, with no success, and two have lost their lives in the process." Mazey expresses.

A small pause as both Mazey and Paul take in the brief encounter with the Colonel. Paul, in his own mind, processing the first day and morning he had. Murder, strange house, strange occurrences, strange townsfolk, and now a secret military base. He ponders, what in the hell has he signed up for, as he awaits the next order from Mazey. The silence is broken up by a knock at the door. "Come in!" Mazey shouts. The door opens and Ranger Evers walks in with a folder in his hand.

"Jesus, Hocho! Why didn't you tell me you crossed the fence when you found the body?" Mazey states emphatically. Hocho walks in and places the folder on her desk. "My people's land before the military took it over. I had to see the body." Hocho replies. "Good morning to both of you by the way." Hocho states, breaking the tension. Mazey cracks a small smile. "Sorry, Paul and I just got our asses chewed out by the Colonel." She explains. "Here are the DNA results you've been waiting on." Hocho says as he sits down.

Mazey opens the file, she quickly reads through the pages. Paul awaits the results. He watches as her eyes go back and forth. Her face begins to squint as if she doesn't like what she sees. She looks up at Hocho. "Did you read this already?" She asks. Hocho smirks. "I gave it a look." Mazey reads the file over again. "Why are there two dead bodies, but we have 3 sets of human DNA and one set of an animal?" She asks the two men. "Not sure Sherrif. Only two dead men at the scene. Mark's body was dragged away." Hocho answers. "Could there have been cross contamination at the scene before we took the bodies?" Paul asks.

Mazey closes the file and puts it down. "The samples were taken from the bodies at the morgue, inside the wounds themselves, and the fur that was inside those wounds." Mazey explains. "Do you have any suspects at all?" Hocho asks. "Just a tall man and some naked townsfolk." Mazey states. Paul and Hocho look at her, intrigued at her statement. "May had a call last night and one this morning about people seeing naked men on their properties. Between Alice's description, believing she thinks it was the man who owns the wood shop, and these other calls we have two options. Go speak with the woodshop owner, Mr. Chaney. Otherwise, we are looking for an insane nudist colony run amuck." Paul smirks, "Both seem like good places to start." He says.

Mazey stands up and addresses them. "Paul and I will go pay a visit to the woodshop and Mr. Chaney. Hocho, go see if you can trace Joey

Marx exit away from the campsite to the plunge spot into the river. Maybe there will be some clues along that trail that could help. Please, as a friend, and a valuable member of this team, stay out of the base. I do not want to lose you or see you arrested by those over-zealous soldiers. Ask around to see if there is such a nudist colony in the area. We all know there are some strange folks up in them hills." Hocho stands and nods in agreement. "As you wish, Sheriff." Hocho nods to Paul and Mazey again, then exits the office. Paul stands and smiles at Mazey. "Let's go find us a tall man."

Chapter 11 Animal Heads

Mazey and Paul ride in her truck near the edge of town. They drive over a large bridge overlooking the Thompson river. Mazey makes a turn down a small dirt road. A sign just in front reads "Chaney Woodworks & Taxidermy." The road is rough and almost covered by the growing trees that surround it. A large metal building and scrap yard appear at the end of the road. A few cars adorn the dirt covered parking lot. The rest of the area is filled with lumber, steel, and large carved statues of animals. They find a parking area and come to a stop. Paul looks at the building and gets a strong uneasy feeling about it. "This looks straight out of a horror movie." He states. Mazey stares at the building as well, slowly remembering the last time she was here. "Wait till you see inside. Last time I was here was when I was thirteen. My dad shot a huge buck during season and brought it here to get taxidermy. I hated that thing. Always felt like it was still alive." Mazey says. She opens the door and the two get out of the vehicle. They walk to a small white door in the center of the building and open it.

It looks so much bigger inside, and creepier. The sound of an electric saw was buzzing in the distance, and the mixed smell of shaved wood, burning sap, and the rotting flesh of animal hides mixed with the morning breeze. Machines and piles of wood, shavings and equipment fill the middle of the room. One of the large walls was covered with hundreds of animal heads and bodies. Paul and Mazey take it all in. There is an eeriness that is thick and uncomfortable. Paul is fixed on all the different animals stuffed and mounted on the wall. A man turns a machine off as he sees the two of them. He wipes his hands and begins to walk toward Mazey and Paul. He was dirty and appeared as if he had lived up in the hills his whole life. He got close to Paul and Mazey and stopped, turning his head, he spit a wad of tobacco juice into a trash can that is nearby. "How can I help ya's?" He says in a strong backwoods accent.

Mazey moves her jacket to show her badge. "I'm Sheriff Keller, this is Deputy Weather. We were hoping to speak to Mr. Chaney, the owner. Is he available?" She asks. The man wipes the sweat off his forehead with a dirty rag from his pocket. "He is on vacation." He states. "When did he leave? When will he be back?" Mazey asks. The man spits more tobacco juice in the trash can and wipes his mouth. "Left this morning, won't be back for a month. He always takes October off. It's his hunting season."

"What is your name, sir?" Paul asks. "I'm Cliff, I'm the shop manager." Cliff responds. "Is there a way we can get a hold of him? A phone number we can reach him at?" Mazey asks. "I'm sorry, when he goes hunting, he requests not to be disturbed. He don't leave us a number to call. He just shows back up on November 1st." Cliff answers. "When was the last time you saw him or spoke to him?" Paul asks. "Night before last. We went over all orders and instructions like we always do before he leaves." Cliff responds. "You mind if we look around a bit? Then we will be out of your hair." Mazey politely asks. "Do it at your own risk. There are a lot of dangerous things scattered around this shop." Cliff informs. "We will be careful and thank you for your time." Mazey responds. "There is a small office in the corner, if you want to leave your card or a note, he can read it and call you when he gets back." Cliff lets the two of them know. "Thank you for your help, sir." Paul says.

The two continue on through the maze of machines, machine parts, wood, animal fragments, dust and sharp objects that seem to be everywhere. The eyes of the dead heads that cover the large wall seem to follow Mazey and Paul as they make their way back to the corner of the building where the small office is. Mazey slowly opens the door. It smells really bad. She covers her nose. "Jesus, what is that concoction?" She asks. The smell hits Paul as well. "Wow, that is a little musky." He replies. The two make their way into the small office. The desk is covered with papers, scattered in no pattern. Animal eyeballs and patches of fur also cover the desk. There are pictures on the wall of Mr. Chaney and other people holding up dead deer, bear, elk, and other prey from their hunting excursions. Mr. Chaney is very tall, towering over everyone else in the pictures. He also resembles the tall man Mazey and Paul saw in the hospital. "It smells like warm cheese and wet dog in here." Mazey states as she looks around to find any clues. Paul stares at the pictures. "Doesn't that look like the wounded man we passed in the hospital?" He asks. Mazey looks at the pictures. "It does." She responds." Paul quickly scours the desk for something. Mazey's eyes focus on a small paper plate in the corner that has molding cheese and sausage on it. Paul spots what he is looking for and quickly grabs a piece of paper off the pile of papers. He looks it over and smiles. "Got it!" He states. Mazey turns to see what Paul has. "What did you find?" She asks and looks at the paper he is holding.

"Looks like a receipt from yesterday morning for treatment at Moorehouse Medical Center." Mazey grabs the paper from him and looks it over. "Says here he was treated for some kind of stabbing or gunshot wound. Dr. Milton was the physician. Perfect! He was on my dad's bowling team. He will tell us." Mazey states. She quickly folds up the paper and puts it in her pocket. "Let's go to the hospital." She says and starts to leave the office. "Are you sure we can take that as evidence?" Paul asks. Mazey stops and looks at the messy desk. "You really think he is going to know its missing?" She asks. Paul looks at the massive clutter in the office. "Good point." He states. The two leave the office and make their way back out of the building, both keeping an eye on the hundreds of animal eyes staring at them from the wall. "Imagine how creepy this place is at night." Paul states. Mazey just shakes her head and keeps her eyes focused on the exit. "Way too many animal heads!" She says.

Chapter 12 Dr. Milton

The door reads "Dr. Walter Milton Chief of Surgery." Mazey and Paul sit inside his office awaiting his arrival. Paul looks at the many degrees and awards adorning the walls of the office. "It was a while ago, but I believe Dr. Milton was the surgeon that replaced my dad's knee." Mazey states while they wait. "It seems like he has the credentials." Paul replies. Dr. Milton walks in. "Sorry, Sheriff for keeping you waiting. How can I help you?" Dr. Milton apologizes as he walks around the two of them and stands behind his desk. Mazey stands up and Paul follows her lead. "Dr. Milton, we will make this brief. This is my new deputy, Paul Weather." Mazey introduces. "Pleasure to meet you, deputy." Dr. Milton extends a greeting. "Doctor!" Paul responds.

"As you know we are currently investigating an attack that happened in the national park. We have evidence to believe that a man suspected in the incident you may have treated recently." Mazey states. Dr Milton shuffles with some papers on his desk. "You believe I treated him?" He asks. "He would have been in here a couple days ago. A real tall man who owns the woodshop and taxidermy on the edge of town. Goes by Lonnie Chaney." Mazey adds. Dr. Milton tries to recall, considering the number of patients he does treat on a daily basis. "Oh, yes, the giant Chaney boy. I have been treating him for years. Very accident prone. He said he had another hunting accident."

"Another hunting accident?" Paul asks. Dr. Milton chuckles a little. "His family are the premiere hunters in this region and have been for generations. His dad and grandfather started the taxidermy business. I have treated Mr. Chaney and his dad several times with all kinds of wounds, like gunshots, deep gashes, bites. I guess hunting can be a dangerous business when you are going after big game." Mazey looks at Paul, the evidence seems to be shining a light on Mr. Chaney. "Did he say how the gun shot happened?" Mazey asks. Dr. Milton pauses again, trying to remember his conversation. "I'm not really sure, he mentioned being up on a ridge and something may have ricochet. He thought it was a stone at first, but it was a bullet." Milton states. "Have you reported this to my office? You do know all gun accidents need to be reported to the Sheriff's department?" Mazey explains.

Dr. Milton opens a drawer in his desk. "I'm sure I informed the hospital administrator, but I will check with her to see if it was done." He pulls out the fragment of the bullet he removed from the drawer and places it on his desk. "You can take this back to the office and file it through evidence if you like." Mazey grabs the bullet fragment and looks it over. "Why did you clean it?" Dr. Milton smiles, "Sorry, force of habit." Mazey hands the bullet to Paul who examines it. "Did you take any blood samples from Mr. Chaney, and if you did, does the lab still have them?" Paul asks. Mazey and Paul stare at the doctor awaiting his answer. He tries to give them a faint smile, trying not to be offended or act guilty in any way.

"I will have the lab send any samples over to you first thing in the morning. Will that be okay Sheriff? Milton asks. Mazey takes the bullet back from Paul and puts it in her pocket. "We appreciate your cooperation, Doctor. If you hear from Mr. Chaney for any reason, please notify me. I would like to have a conversation with him and see if there is any correlation between this attack in the park and his current incident." Mazey says and smiles politely. Dr. Milton smiles back. "Absolutely, Sheriff, you will have my full cooperation." Mazey taps

Paul on the shoulder. "We will get out of your hair then; we know you are a busy man." Mazey walks out of the office. Paul nods to the doctor and follows Mazey out. Dr. Milton waits till they leave, then breathes a deep breath of relief and sits in his chair. He pulls out his phone and dials a number.

Chapter 13 New Evidence

Downtown Forest River Hill is almost complete and ready for the Fall Festival. The streets and shops are decorated, and hay bales and pumpkins adorn the entrances to most shops. Banners and signs clutter the streets of the square. Mazey sits at a table in Bigfoot's Café trying to enjoy her food in peace. The front doorbell chimes as Riley Forest walks in. She has a determined look on her face as she peers around the restaurant. She spies Mazey and takes a beeline to her table. Mazey, a little upset that her meal is about to be interrupted, sighs, and puts her fork down hard. "I figured you would be here." Riley opens with. "Is there any way whatso ever that this can wait Riley?" Mazey asks in frustration. Riley disregards her and sits down.

"I'll be brief, but I thought you might want to know that I have released Matt White and Al Thorn from the hospital. I would like to set up a time in the next week to have them come in with me and provide an official statement. I believe both of them are innocent and have clear evidence that this was an animal attack." Riley states. "Get with May to schedule the times, but we have some new evidence that could contradict their story, so we will see." Mazey explains. Riley sits up in her chair in light of this new position from Mazey. "New evidence? How new?" She asks.

"You know the woodwork and taxidermy place at the end of town?" Mazey asks. "The Chaney's place, yes." Riley answers. "Well apparently, Lonnie was treated for a bullet wound by Dr. Milton the morning after the incident in the park." Mazey states. "What does that have to do with Matt and Al?" Riley asks. "Matt, Joe, and Al all reported that whatever attacked them was very tall, which Mr. Chaney is. Seven foot tall or more from files reported." Mazey responds. "Is there any evidence placing him at the scene? Does he have an alibi? What about all the animal hair that was found on all the victims?"

Mazey takes a sip of her drink, not enjoying the questions from Riley. "I would love to answer those questions. When we went to see Mr. Chaney at his place of business, we were informed he would be gone for the entire month hunting. As far as animal hair goes, we all know Mr. Chaney has access to hundreds of animal pelts since that is what he does. It would be easy for him to drape himself in a bear or wolf skin and be at that scene." Mazey states. "Will you be putting an APB out for him?" Riley asks.

"We will be putting the bullet fragment Dr. Milton provided through forensics to see if it matches the gun used at the park. So more than likely, yes, we will put out an APB." Riley pauses, realizing Mazey just wants to enjoy her lunch. "Where is your new Deputy?" She asks. "Paul is at the station, working on the case." Mazey responds. Riley smiles at Mazey as if she is being too brief. "How are things going with Paul? Riley inquires. "Good, he seems very capable, so far. He has good intuition." Mazey answers. Riley smiles again, "He's also kind of handsome, don't you think?"

Mazey shakes her head, knowing were Riley is trying to go with this. Riley has always played matchmaker with her, and most have been misses. "Be real Riley. You know I don't shit where I eat!" she responds. "Obviously. I'm just glad he is working out. I know how bad you needed help." Riley adds. "Can I finish my meal now?" Mazey asks. "Absolutely, I have some cases I need to get to as well." Riley collects herself and stands up. "Just get your clients to me this week and we will see if their story changes with this new evidence." Mazey remarks. "I'll get with May and get it on the books. I hope you find Mr. Chaney. Tell Paul, I said hello."

"I'll do you one better, I'll give him your number and let him know you are terribly desperate for a date." Mazey jests. Riley smiles at the idea. "That's not too far away from the truth." She states. She waves goodbye and heads back out of the restaurant.

Chapter 14 The Wine and the Fish

Night has fallen, and Paul lays in bed, the black book given to him by Nadia lays on his bent knees. He adjusts his glasses as he turns the page. His mind races with intrigue as the unique pictures of werewolves, strange symbols and ancient stories fill each page. He wonders if any of this is possible. Being a man of faith makes it seem like such nonsense. Paul also realizes that demons can come in all shapes and sizes. Who is to say that these creatures are not the fallen angels the bible discusses? The small bedside lamp barely fills the room with light. His eyes begin to get heavy and worn from the words and images page after page. He removes his glasses and lays the book on the side table. He rubs his eyes, yawns, and sits still. Thoughts continue to fill him, as he takes in the silence.

Quickly he lifts his head. From outside the bedroom door the sound of footsteps on the stairs fills the air, similar to the ones he heard on the first day in the house. He slowly gets out of the bed. He opens the side table drawer where his side arm sits. He slowly takes it out of the drawer and walks toward the bedroom door. The footsteps stop. Paul stops. A door creeks.

"Hello?" Paul says loudly so the intruder knows he is awake and aware. He waits for a response. He holds the gun steady in front of him and walks towards the hall. He turns the corner to the hall. It is dark, but the light from the downstairs kitchen shines a soft glow. Nobody is in the hall. He looks down to see that the room on the right at the top of the stairs is open. Methodically Paul opens the doors of each room upstairs, turning on the light, and investigating each room. Once the room is clear, he turns off the light. Making it to the final room, which is open already, he peers into the darkness of the room, spying for any movement, or any shadow to manifest. "This is Deputy Paul Weather. I am armed." He announces before he moves forward into the room. He aims steadily. He quickly removes one hand from the gun and turns on the light in the room. No one is there. He breathes a sigh of relief and lowers his gun. He turns off the light and turns his attention to the stairs. There doesn't appear to be any imprints of a foot or shoe on the stairs. He peers down to the living room, and all is still and quiet.

Maybe it was his imagination. The book he was reading was enough to make your mind wander.

Suddenly, behind Paul, a figure in a dress moves from the room across from his bedroom and into the bedroom. Paul turns to go back, but the figure is already in the bedroom. Paul walks back to the bedroom and inside. There is no one in the room. Paul puts the gun back in the side drawer and walks into the bathroom to brush his teeth. Behind Paul in the corner of the room a woman in an old beige dress walks to the chair and sits down. She has long beautiful blonde hair, seems to be in her late twenties, with a thin gaunt face. Paul spits out the toothpaste and washes out his mouth. He looks up. The mirrors reflection reveals the chair, but no woman sitting in it. He rinses his mouth again, spits, and wipes his face. He stares at himself in the mirror for a moment, unaware of the visitor awaiting his return. "Hey, Riley, funny running into you here." He says quietly. Laughs at himself and dismisses the insane thought.

Paul walks over to the chair in the corner and takes off his shirt. He lays it on the back of the chair and walks back to the bed. He gets inside, makes himself comfortable and turns off the light. "Thank you, Jesus, for a good night's sleep." He prays silently, then positions himself to sleep. The room is still and quiet, not even the sound of nature outside. Paul begins to drift off.

'Chaney!' Suddenly a voice quietly from the other side of the room fills the air.

He quickly opens his eyes and sits up. Paul looks around the room in the dark trying to glimpse anything. His head turns to the chair, and he is surprised as he sees what looks like a female silhouette sitting in it. He quickly turns on the light. And sees that the only thing there is his shirt. He takes a deep breath and relaxes. Turning back to the light, he turns it off and nestles himself back under the covers and tries to sleep.

'Chaney!' rings out once again from the other side of the room. Paul quickly jumps up, turns on the light and peers over to the chair. Again, the shirt is the only item on the chair. Paul stares at the chair, breathing heavily. He slowly lowers his breath and calms his nerves. "Note to self, don't read scary books before bed." He laughingly says out loud. Paul once again returns to bed. Turning off the light and covering himself in the sheets and the blanket. His breathing slows. He closes his eyes, then opens them, maybe awaiting something else. Slowly his tiredness draws his eyelids closed, his body relaxes, and he begins to fall back to sleep.

The air is still. His body is still. He begins to fade. Slowly, he feels a hand and arm come across his shoulder and lay over his chest. His eyes fling open. He feels the arm. He sees the arm. 'Help me.' The same voice whispers. Paul screams and jumps out of the bed. He fumbles to turn on the light. There is nothing in the bed. His heart is racing. "Jesus, what is happening?" He shouts and asks himself. He looks around the room. Again, nothing or no one is in there with him. He puts his hand on his waist and takes a couple deep breaths to lower his heart rate. "It was the wine, and the fish!" he says to himself as his breath and heart rate slows down. Stillness and quietness set in, and Paul relaxes.

A door downstairs slams shut. Paul jumps. He quickly gets the gun back out of the drawer and races out of the room. He runs down the hall and down the stairs to the first floor. He aims the gun in front of him and searches around the room for any sign of an intruder. There is no one in the living room and the front door is shut. He sees that the deadbolt is locked. Paul walks into the kitchen and investigates. Nothing is out of place in the kitchen. He does a complete three-sixty turn one more time. Out of the corner of his eye he notices the door in the dining room leading outside is open. He rushes over to the door, aiming toward the porch. He stops suddenly. Peering out into the back yard, heading toward the stream and forest he sees what looks like a woman in a dress. He quickly makes his way to the door and out onto the back porch. The woman walks directly toward the forest.

Paul walks down the porch stairs and into the yard. He lowers his gun and watches the woman walk. "Hello!" He shouts, attempting to get her attention. The woman passes the shed and begins walking through the stream. "Can I help you?" he shouts. He walks a few feet into the yard towards her. He isn't sure if this is a vision or an actual person. He continues to watch as she passes the stream and walks into the forest, slowly disappearing. Suddenly, Paul raises the gun with two hands, the hairs on his arms stand up. From the forest, where the lady walked, appears the two large red eyes. The same as he saw the other night. Paul sharply aims in that direction.

"What in the hell?" he softly asks himself. Coming out of the brush was a large wolflike creature on all fours. It was wide, with dark hair, and eyes glowing. The animal's firm breath can be seen in the cold night. It stopped at the edge of the creek and stared at Paul. Paul's breath and heart rate start to rise again. It's dark, but the beast seems clear to him. He tries to keep a steady hand and a steady aim at the beast. The animal growls at him and shows his large jaw and sharp bloody teeth. Paul cocks his gun and readies to fire if the animal comes forward. Suddenly the animal stands on its hind legs, like a bear would do, and howls loudly at the night sky. Paul walked a few feet towards it ready to fire.

"Chaney!" Paul shouts toward the animal. The beast comes back down on all fours, snarls again at Paul. It slowly turns its body and walks back into the forest. Paul watches as it totally disappears. He finally lowers his gun. In his weariness and fright, Paul sits down on the lawn and tries to catch his breath. "It's definitely the wine and the fish." He says again to himself.

Chapter 15: It's a Date Then

The Forest River Hill Town Hall is full of residents. The annual fall festival meeting always draws a majority of the townsfolk to discuss what they like and dislike about the festival. The shop owners are represented, and Riley is there for the café. Mayor Moorhouse is up front at the podium running the short event. Mazey and Paul stood on the side of the stage along with the rest of their staff. May sat on the front row.

"We want to thank Rick Hutchinson with Hutchinson Honda for supplying his parking lot at the dealership for all of the overflow parking. We also want to thank him for his sponsorship and for providing the vans to transport guests back and forth to the square." The Mayor continues his announcements. "There will be golf carts making rounds all day to pick up trash and to deliver supplies to all the vendors. Please make sure you turn in your list to the council by Thursday." Mayor Morehouse looks over to Mazey to signal that she is next. "This will be a fabulous festival; ticket sales are fantastic. We expect a good amount of traffic to all of your businesses. Thank you for your time this evening. We will close with Sheriff Keller, who will discuss security, and where the stations will be this year. Thank you everyone, and please give your attention to Sheriff Keller." The Mayor said as he left the podium. He shook hands with Mazey as she walked to the podium to speak.

"Thank you, Mayor Moorehouse. I'll make this brief; I know everyone wants to get home to their families. We will have three manned stations, and they will be located outside the library, Nadia's, and Bigfoot's Café. We will have two EMT teams roaming throughout the day and night. Like I have said every year, please, if you see anything strange, call the Sheriff's hotline and report it. My Deputy Paul Weather and I will be at the festival every day." Mazey looks at the crowd and sees Alice Higgins with her hand raised. Mazey sighs, knowing this is probably not going to be good. "How can I help you, Alice?" Mazey cautiously asks. Alice stands up. "When you say strange, does that include all the naked people that have been seen running around town?" The audience moans and murmurs with her announcement. The very question Mazey was afraid would be asked. "Alice, I assure you there will not be any naked people at the festival, but yes, if you see anyone acting strange, please call the hotline." Mazey answers. Another citizen stands up, encouraged by Alice's question and shouts to the Sheriff up front. "What about this rumor of a giant animal running wild in the park?" Mazey, now annoyed, turns to Paul, and motions him to come over. Paul slowly walks to the podium.

"Folks, this is a rumor, there is no large animal in the park. We have confirmed this, as well as Ranger Evers with the National Park service. Let's end this meeting on a positive note. The fall festival is the favorite event of the year next to the Nativity Parade. Our children and their families enjoy the rides, venues, and prizes. Let us make it a fun, memorable and safe time for everyone. This meeting is adjourned, I hope everyone has a safe trip home." Mazey leaves the podium and directs Paul to follow her offstage.

As the crowd stands and begins to talk amongst themselves, forming their familiar circles. May takes a beeline to Alice to help her out of the hall, and to keep her from stirring up the citizens. Mazey and Paul walk around the backside of the hall away from the citizens. "Every year Alice has to ask something that stirs up the crowd. Last year she spread a rumor that there was a radical religious group that was going to blockade the road coming into town during the festival." Mazey remarks. Walking down the back wall coming toward them is a tall gentleman, a white-haired, kind-faced citizen. "You've been spotted." Mazey says to Paul under her breath. The man reaches his hand out to Paul.

"Welcome to the great City of Forest River Hill Deputy Weather's" The man says. Paul reaches out and shakes his hand. "Good to see you Sheriff." He addresses Mazey. "Good to see you, Pastor." Mazey replies. "Pastor Gary Hill, pleasure to meet you, Paul." Gary says. Paul returns the greeting, "Nice to meet you, Pastor."

"Sheriff, I just wanted you to know that if you need any extra rooms or space, you are more than welcome to a few of our classrooms at the church, you can use our parking lot as well if you need extra overflow." Gary advices Mazey. "We appreciate that, Pastor; I will let you know if we do require more space. If you will excuse me though, I have to catch the Mayor before he leaves." Mazey explains. "Absolutely, don't let me keep you." Gary responds. "I'll see you back at the station, Paul." Mazey states as she walks away. Leaving Paul alone with Gary.

"What church do you pastor?" Paul asks. "Forest River Hill Christian Fellowship. We are a non-denominational church. My grandfather established it in 1942. My father took it over in 1992, and I took it over in 2022." Gary answers. "I'll have to come to service one Sunday." Paul responds. "We would love to see you. Anytime you would like a tour of the campus, please stop by and I'd love to show you the history of the church." Gary invites. Paul's attention is diverted as he sees Riley walking toward them. He notices how pretty she is. He had thought that at the café, but tonight it is being confirmed. Riley walks up behind Gary and puts her arm around him.

"Pastor Gary, may I interrupt you quickly?" She states. Gary turns and smiles when he sees who it is. "Riley, absolutely, so good to see you." Gary responds. "Councilman Logan wanted a few minutes of your time before you left. He said it was about the building expansion." Riley explains. "Yes, I've been waiting to visit. Please excuse me, Deputy. Swing by the church anytime, I would love to visit more." Gary says, as he quickly excuses himself to catch the councilman. Paul watches Gary walking away. He turns to look at Riley who stares at him with a quirky smile on her face. "Councilman Logan isn't here still, is he?" Paul asks. Riley smiles big. "I believe he left already. Mazey told me to come save you from Pastor Gary." She answers. "I appreciate that." Paul gratefully responds. "So, deputy, how have things been?" Riley asks. "A little crazy, maybe hectic, but not boring." Paul responds. "We are so happy you're here. I especially. Mazey works so hard, and I'm glad she has someone to help her carry some of the load." Riley responds. "She has been very supportive and helpful. Having a murder case on your first day can be overwhelming, but she has been solid the whole time." Paul states.

The two pause their conversation. Not an awkward pause, but just taking a moment and studying each other's eyes and presence. Both are engaged in the moment. Riley breaks the silence. "I know you will be working the festival, but will you have any time to actually enjoy it and walk around exploring?" She asks. "I'm sure I will. My understanding is we are pretty much on call the whole day, but unless something major happens, I should have some down time." Paul answers. "If you do get time and you would like a tour guide, let me know. This will be my 30th fall festival I will be attending. I know all the great spots, 'and' the best treats. If you like beer, there is a booth that makes a delicious pumpkin-maple stout." Riley notes.

"That sounds amazing. Very kind of you to offer your expertise." Paul responds. "I'll be at the café. We make our "Sasquatch Cinnamon Rolls," which four people can feed on just one." Riley states. "How can I say no to seasonal craft beer and gigantic pastries? Let alone a tour from a 'third-generation citizen'." Paul remarks. Riley smiles at his subtle wit. "Shall we call it a date then?" Riley asks. "As long as there is no dance at the end of this date. Unfortunately, I have two left feet." Paul quirks. "No dance, but would you be opposed to a hayride down to the river?" Riley suggests. "I'm not opposed to a hayride." Paul confirms. "That settles it deputy, it's a date then. Make sure you tell Mazey I did rescue you. I'll see you at the festival." Riley smiles. She glances at Paul, so glad that Mazey sent her to have this moment. She then walks away and back into the hall. Paul watches her leave, and a small smile forms on his face as well. "It's a date, then." He says quietly to himself.

Chapter 16: What Happened in the Woods?

The day had come. What happened in the woods? This was the question Mazey and Paul would be asking, Joey Marx, Matt White, and Al Thorn. Between the incident, Paul beginning, Hocho violating the Military bases border, and the discovery of Mr. Chaney's bullet wound, the case seemed like it had stalled a bit. Mazey was anxious to hear from the remaining men who survived the attack that night. Hopefully, they have had time to recover from their wounds, and possibly recall in more detail what actually happened.

Sitting in a plain, unassuming private room, with cameras in the corner of the roof, a small table with chairs on either side, Mazey, Paul, Matt and Riley look across from each other. Mazey has files and pictures of the incident in front of her. Riley sits across not as Mazey's childhood friend, but the defense counsel for the accused. Matt White still has the deep scratches across his face from the animal. "Mr. White, is it still your understanding that you and the other men that were with you in the park were attacked by some large wild animal?" Mazey asks. She continues, "I will be asking Joey Marx and Al Thorn the same questions today just to make sure we get a real understanding of how each of you perceives the event." She looks at the picture of the dead body of Bill. "Just tell me briefly, your version of what happened." She asks.

Matt sits up in his chair and leans forward a bit to begin. "We were up there celebrating our second softball championship. We were having a good time, talking about the game and life. We heard the sound of something in the woods. Bill pulled out his firearm just in case. The sounds went away, and we all just chuckled about it. Then we heard the growl from behind Bill. Before we could react, the animal attacked Bill from behind. Bill pulled the trigger, and the gun shot Al in the leg. Joey ran off immediately. I believe Larry went for his bag to get a gun. The animal jumped off Bill and onto Al and began attacking him. Mark and I grabbed whatever we could and ran to Al to see if we could beat the animal off of him." Matt stopped. His breath heavy, his mind remembering the scene, he then continued, "Before we could get to Al, the animal turned and stood. It towered over us, and before we could strike, it knocked Mark and I to the ground. My face felt like it had been ripped off."

"When you say it stood up, do you mean like a man would stand up, or like a bear?" Mazey quickly asks. Matt sits back again in the chair, not understanding Mazey's intent. "I don't really remember. It just turned and rose. It was dark, and we just had the firelight, but it hovered over us quickly and knocked us both out." He explains. "So, you can't really say for sure if it was or wasn't a man, since the light was dim?" Mazey asks. Riley gives her a look, as if to be careful. Matt shakes his head, trying to remember clearly. "It didn't look like a man. It was covered in dark fur, it growled and snarled, and its teeth were like that of a canine." He answers.

"Are you sure the alcohol wasn't flowing too hard, and you all had a disagreement? Maybe tempers flared and y'all began firing at each other?" Mazey asks firmly. "Don't answer that, Matt!" Riley quickly interrupts. "May I remind you Sheriff that we are not in a courtroom. I will not have you baiting my client. He is here to give you a statement of the events that occurred that night. Keep your questions to the event or we will leave right now and see you in court." Riley concludes. Paul writes something down on the paper in front of him. Riley notices it and looks at him.

Mazey gives Riley a stern look, but knows she is not playing around.

"Mr. White, do you remember what happened to Mark Roberts?" Mazey asks. Matt takes a deep breath. He becomes emotional as he speaks. "The animal left. I thought it was gone. I could hear Al moaning in pain, but I couldn't hear Mark. A few minutes later the animal returned and stood over me. I assumed I was next, so I just closed my eyes and prayed. The next thing I remember was waking up in the hospital. I didn't know what happened to the rest." Mazey sat back, not sure how sincere Matt was being. "Matt, do you remember Larry firing his weapon at the animal, and if he hit it?" Paul speaks up. Matt stares at Paul, remembering he did hear another gunshot. "I believe I heard two shots. I was on the ground at that time and did not see if he hit it." Matt answers. Paul continues to write on his paper. "Was Lonnie Chaney with you men that night?" Mazey asks. Matt looks confused. "The taxidermist on the edge of town? No, he isn't on the softball team." Matt responds. Riley sternly stares at Mazey. "Are we good?" "For now, but I suggest you instruct your client not to leave town." Mazey commands.

It's 10:00 am, and Al Thorn now sits across from Mazey and Paul. Riley stands by, to advise the next man who lived through that horrible night. Mazey stares at Al whose face is still scarred and battered. "Al, do you know why Bill shot you?" Mazey asks directly. "Careful, Sheriff. Wrong phrasing." Riley interrupts and corrects her. "Sorry, counsel. Al, how and when did you get shot in the leg?" Mazey rephrases.

Al turns to Riley, making sure it is okay to answer. Riley nods to continue. "We had heard something in the woods. Bill was being silly and drew his rifle, acting as if he was going to shoot something in the woods. The sounds went away for a bit, but then came back. Bill was aiming at something behind Larry. The animal must have circled the campsite because moments later it attacked Bill from behind. His hand must have been on the trigger because the gun went off and the bullet hit me in my chair." Al answers. "Bill and Larry weren't having an argument? Are you sure Bill didn't intend to shoot Larry?" Mazey asks. Riley upset again, quickly interrupts, "Sheriff! My client cannot possibly understand the intent of another man. Please refrain from those questions."

"Did you see who or what Larry shot at?" Paul asks. Al shakes his head. Trying to remember after the shot from Bill. "All I remember is the pain from the shot. Bill was screaming. I tried to move out of the chair. I think that was what drew the animal's attention. Next thing I knew it leaped on me and knocked me down. It was clawing and biting my chest, but the only pain I could still feel was the gunshot wound. I was sure it was going to kill me. It got off of me and turned around. Right before I passed out, I heard gun shots, but I didn't see where they hit." Al takes a deep breath; the remembering is upsetting. He wipes the tears from his eyes. "I awoke in the hospital, and I had no idea if anyone else had survived."

Mazey sees the sincerity in Al's emotions. "One last question, Al. Did you see Lonnie Chaney anywhere in the park that night?" Mazey asks. Riley gives her another stern look. Al looks confused. "No, what does Lonnie have to do with this?" Al asks. Riley interrupts, "I think he described his experience that night. This will be the end of the interview." Mazey leans back in her chair and shrugs at Riley.

The clock hits the eleven am hour. A nervous Joey Marx sits next to Riley. Mazey and Paul rub their eyes, understanding this is a bit of a beating. The stories are not giving any clues as to what might have happened that night that would lead to anything other than an animal. Mazey leans in. Her brief interaction with Joey the morning after the attack was now fuzzy since so many other things have happened. "Mr. Marx, the one who got away, and dove into the river. Tell me, why were you the only one that ran away?"

Joey slowly rocks back and forth in the chair, staring back and forth at Mazey and Paul. "We were having a great time. We were all happy that we had won back-to-back championships. The first howl we heard, everyone seemed to ignore, and I believe Al made a joke about it being Larry's wife. I knew right away that howl sounded different. My Uncle Roy rescued wolves that the pack left behind. I grew up hearing wolves. There was something different in the tone and pitch of that howl." Paul writes something down in his notes. Joey continues, "With each howl we heard, I knew it was getting closer. The boys were just joking around. Maybe the beers had finally caught up to us. When Bill started waving his rifle around, I became a little concerned." Mazey sat up.

"Why were you concerned? Did Bill seem agitated by anyone? Did he seem threatening?" Mazey asked. Joey, still nervous, wipes the sweat off his forehead. "Bill is a nice guy; I don't believe he would ever hurt any of us. I was just concerned that he may have had too much to drink and alcohol and loaded weapons are never a good combination. The final howl was a hideous sound. I could tell how close the animal was. I didn't have a gun with me like the others, so I knew if the animal did attack, I may have to flee." Joey states. "When did you actually run?" Paul asks.

Joey, remembering the moment, shakenly describes the moment he ran. "I saw the beast the moment it attacked Bill from behind. It was enormous. It was more the size of a bear than a wolf, but the howl and its snout was of a wolf. As soon as Bill's gun went off and I heard Al scream, I ran. I ran for my life!" Mazey leans in and looks at Joey. "So, you weren't really there and saw what happened? You can't say for sure if it were an animal? Could it have been a person in a fur coat that attacked everyone?" She asks. Joey slows his breathing down. He stares at Mazey and Paul. "You want to know how I know it was an animal

Sheriff?" He asks. Mazey leans back in her seat. "Yes, please tell me how for sure, you know it was an animal." Mazey asks.

Joey takes a deep breath and then explains. "You and Riley will remember, because we all grew up here and went to the same High School. My junior and senior year I won state in the hundred- and two-hundred-meter races. There aren't too many people in these parts that can catch me. I had a good thirty-second head start into the woods, and probably had a two-to-three-hundred-yard lead before I heard that animal come after me. No man alive I know could have made up the ground that that beast made up in such a short time. When I hit the edge of the cliff, it was less than a hundred feet away from me. I did the only thing I knew I could, which was to jump. When I came up to the surface, looked up at the cliff, it was no man standing there. Whatever that thing is, it is bigger, faster, and stronger than any man that was there that night. The fact that Matt and Al are alive, is a miracle." A calm goes over the room. There is no lie in the words that were just spoken. Everyone could feel that.

"I think we will end there. Sheriff, I believe you got the testimony of these men today and what happened that night. I'm sure you will make the right decision going forward. Joey, we can leave now." Riley states as Joey and she stands up. Mazey, upset, slams her pen on the table. Riley and Joey begin to walk out of the room, Joey stops and addresses Mazey and Paul. "I hope you believe me. That thing is still out there. Until you find it, no one in this town is safe." He walks out, Riley motions for Mazey to call her, then she leaves with Joey. Mazey and Paul look at each other. Knowing all three men had pretty similar stories, and no real thread to a murder by human hands. "I still feel like something is missing, or these men are not telling the whole truth." Mazey states.

Paul is torn. He has seen a creature twice now. He isn't sure if it is his imagination, or if these men saw the same thing he saw. At this point he does not feel comfortable to share with Mazey. He remains silent and avoids any contamination of this case. "I say we get Hocho, and the three of us do another examination of the campsite. Maybe we missed something. It wouldn't hurt after hearing their stories." Paul says. Mazey takes in his suggestion. "You're probably right. Let me contact Hocho and see when he can meet us." Mazey agrees. "Riley is tough, isn't she?" She adds. Paul smiles, he was impressed with her today. "She is a bit intimidating." He adds.

Chapter 17: Thank God for Trees

The campsite will never be the same. The rain and coroner's unit cleaned up as much as it could, but the memories and terror still reside over the ground the blood of those men painted. The police tape still surrounds the scene of the crime. Mazey, Hocho and Paul each walk slowly in different spots of the campsite. "Larry fired two shots. We have the one bullet that was found in Chaney, and hopefully forensics will be able to have the results tomorrow. We need to find the other shot that was fired and get that through forensics as well." Mazey announces. Paul walks through a patch of trees just off the campsite in the direction of Larry's shot. He scopes out the ground, the shrubs, and the trees for any signs or evidence. The sun peers through an opening in the canopy and catches Paul in the eyes. He squints and turns away. When his vision comes back in full just in front of him, he sees something reflecting the sun inside a tree just ahead.

He arrives to the tree, leans in, and realizes it is a bullet lodged inside the bark. 'Sheriff!" He shouts. Mazey and Hocho hear and turn. They see him away from the campsite in a grove of trees. "Over here!" He shouts again. Mazey and Hocho rush over to him as Paul has removed a knife and begins to remove the bullet from the tree. "Great work, Paul." Hocho remarks. "Thank God for trees." Mazey adds. Paul manages to get the bullet out and he hands it to Mazey. She reviews it, looking at the size and shape of it. She looks at Paul. "It sure looks similar to the one we got from Dr. Milton." Mazey states. "Hocho, can you lead us down the trail that Joey fled on?" Paul asks. "Sure thing, follow me." Hocho responds.

Mazey and Paul follow Hocho down the trail Joey fled down. The tracks have been washed away by rain, but you can still see were branches were broken by Joey, or whatever was chasing him. They scour the ground and trees searching for any other sign they may have missed. They made it all the way to the edge of the cliff where Joey had to jump. Realizing it took them several minutes to walk, they noted the distance it was from the campsite. Mazey looks over the edge to see how far Joey jumped. "That has to be seventy feet at least. At night it would seem even farther. How scared do you have to be to jump from this height?" Mazey says. "Joey said the animal looked big as he was floating away on the river. If it looked big from down there in the dark, how big was it?" Paul asks. Hocho kneels down and picks up a handful of dirt from the edge and smells it. He stands and looks at the water below. "Halchin Natanik!" He proclaims.

Mazey and Paul turn to him. "What does that mean" Mazey asks. "It translates to 'Moon Dog.' Kootenai Indian legend speaks of a large doglike creature that hunted during the full moon. Some say it is a skin walker. A man who is possessed by an evil spirit and can turn himself into a dog or wolf." Hocho explains. Paul looks back at the trail, imagining the creature he saw at the house could be the same one that attacked those men.

"Sheriff Keller, come in. Over!" They are interrupted by May calling from the station on Mazey's radio. Mazey responds, "Hey, May, this is Keller, over!" "Sheriff, Anthony from the lab just called. He confirmed that the two blood samples, one from the bodies, and the one the hospital sent over are a match. Lonnie Chaney's DNA is confirmed on both samples. Over!" May says. "Thanks, May. We will be back in twenty minutes, over!" May responds. Mazey frustrated, kicks dirt off the edge of the cliff.

"What the hell is going on here? Three men giving testimony of an attack by an animal, and no presence of Lonnie Chaney. Yet, we have DNA that connects him to the bodies, and a bullet taken from his shoulder." Mazey states. "Someone is lying." Hocho remarks. "If that bullet comes back matching Larry's gun, we may have a fugitive on the run." Paul states. Mazey looks one more time at the bullet Paul found. "Thank God for trees!" She remarks.

Chapter 18 Waxing Gibbous

The first night of the Fall Festival has arrived. The streets are full of the townsfolk and several tourists who frequent this festival every year. Children are playing games, eating fall treats, and running around laughing. Adults are partaking of the local spirits and sweetened treats. Shop owners, street performers and artists are hustling their way into extra revenue for the quarter. The Mayor is out shaking hands and asking for votes. Mazey and Paul patrol the streets. The noise is festive and loud, and it travels through the night, which is clear and the perfect backdrop for the Waxing Gibbous moon that gives light to the town and surrounding forest. Just a few blocks from downtown, on the back porch of a small house sits Matt White. He is finishing a cold beer and hamburger, enjoying the peaceful night and the sounds of the festival.

Matt lays his beer and plate on the side table. He leans back in his chair and stares at the clear night, and the moon that seems to glow. A low hum begins in his ears and begins to pulse. It seems to feel like he can hear his heartbeat. Thump, thump! Suddenly he stands and grabs his stomach. The humming and thumping get louder. The noise from the festival disappears. In severe pain, Matt drops to his knees. He lets out a cry of pain. He throws his head forward and begins to throw up, food and blood come pouring from his mouth. He looks down and sees the chewed up digested food covered in a thick dark blood. He lays his hands on the porch to brace for the next round that comes quickly. Again, food and blood. He moans in agony from the pain in his gut.

A deeper scream of agony as he looks down at his hands and in terror, he watches his fingernails begin to grow quickly and sharpen to a point, blood coming from the cuticles. He quickly stands in shock looking at what appears to be claws now, and bloody fingers. He tries to turn around and go inside, but his body gives out and he falls on the porch on his back. His eyes fixed again on the moon and its glow. Suddenly, he hears a growl down below, coming from the bottom of the stairs. He tries to lift his head to see, but his head won't rise. He lowers his eyes to see what he now feels on his foot. A large claw clamps onto his ankle. He screams. His body is slowly dragged off the porch and down the lawn.

Joy reclaims the air as we drift once again across the town square. The lights, the festivity, the memories being made. Paul is breaking up a disagreement with two inebriated adults. Riley is watching from a distance. Through the streets and near the end of the festival, the Mayor and Colonel Riser speak on the steps of the town courthouse. Mazey is watching her children play carnival games and win prizes.

Over the hill and through the woods. Al Thorns house overlooks the river. Al sits in his lazy boy chair in his living room watching a baseball game on television. He devours a bowl of ice cream in his lap. He engulfs a giant spoonful of ice cream filled with chunks of chocolate and cookie dough pieces. He hears a crunch, different from the sound of chocolate chunks.

Removing the spoon from his mouth he notices that the ice cream is covered with blood, and rising from a piece of chocolate is an incisor tooth. Al jumps up from the chair. He grabs the tooth from the bowl. He frantically lifts his finger to his mouth and realizes there is a space in his upper row where a tooth should be. He drops the bowl and hobbles to the bathroom. He panics as he smiles in the mirror and both incisors are gone. His mind is racing with disbelief. He puts his fingers in both empty spaces and screams. Screams of shock and now pain as slowly larger sharper teeth grow out of the spaces. No longer human incisors, but the size and shape of canine fangs. He turns quickly as a loud howl comes from the living room. Slowly, Al, whose ears recognize that sound, walks back into the living room. The front door is open. He scurries over, shuts it, and locks the deadbolt. Another growl comes from deep inside the house.

Down the hall, coming out of a room, Al sees it. The beast. The creature from that night. The only word that goes through his mind is 'Joey.' He realizes he needs to run. He quickly turns, unlocks the front door, opens it, and hobbles as fast as he can out of the house and down through his yard to the river. The sound of the beast gaining ground on him fills the night air. His leg finally gives out and he falls to the ground. He tries to get back up but the pain in his leg and mouth immobilizes him. He can feel the drool from the beast's long snout drop on the back of his neck. Al screams and claws the ground attempting to stop the beast's momentum, but it is too strong. The beast drags him back into the house.

The waxing gibbous continues to romance the sky. As midnight strikes the town square is clear. The streets are empty of people, but filled with the debris, graffiti and trash that litters the street. The lights are mostly out, especially in the shops and restaurants. The one that remains on is Nadia's place. She sits at the counter counting the receipts from the night. On the counter in front of her stands a small oval shaped crystal. As Nadia continues to close the evening she is distracted as the crystal illuminates an amber glow. She immediately stops counting and looks up. Through the store, out the glass window, across the street, down a small dark alley between two buildings, she sees them. The glowing amber eyes of the beast. She stands as the beast reveals his snout and sharp bloody teeth.

Nadia reaches down and lifts up her dress. Holstered and strapped to her knee-high boots is a large silver pistol. She draws it out, lifts it and aims it in the direction of the beast. The beast snarls, but slowly closes its mouth and disappears back in the dark. The crystal dims.

Chapter 19: Hybridization

The following evening, after the festival, Nadia sits again at the counter in her shop adding up the receipts for the day. The front door opens and Mazey walks in, in uniform, finishing her shift at the festival. Nadia pauses what she is doing to greet the Sheriff. "Another successful night for the festival, Sheriff?" Mazey makes her way to the counter. "I would say so, only one drunk for the cell. Farmer Bob won the pumpkin pie eating contest for the third year in a row." Mazey states. "What can I do for you, tonight?" Nadia asks. "I need the key to the cabin. I have a box I need to go through." Mazey states.

Nadia looks at Mazey, she can sense the sadness as she asks for the key. "It never ends does it. Some things never feel solved." Nadia remarks. "My spider senses still tingle." Mazey replies. Nadia nods and gets up from the counter. "I understand, let me get it for you." Nadia walks to the back, through the curtain, into the back room. She makes a beeline to the tall bookshelf with the old books. She reaches and grabs a thick book from the fifth shelf. She opens the book and flips about halfway through it. The back half of the book has a rectangle carved out of the pages, and inside is a large, thick, metal key. A key that appears would open a treasure chest from the fifteen hundreds. She removes the key, closes the book, and places it back on the shelf. She reaches into the glass case, with the weapons, and grabs a small silver bag filled with what would appear to be sand.

Walking back out front, Nadia places the bag on the counter and hands the key to Mazey. "I hope you figure something out tonight." She states. Mazey puts the key in her pocket. "I know I'm getting closer, just missing a few more pieces, I'm sure." Mazey responds. "Be safe driving out there, these roads are dangerous at night." Nadia warns. "I'll bring this back in the morning." Mazey states. Nadia watches as Mazey leaves and heads down the street. Nadia, sensing an eeriness in the night grabs the bag and takes it outside to the front of the store. She cautiously looks down the street, then across the way to the darkened alley she saw the beast last night. She opens the bag, puts in her hand, and pulls out a handful of shiny silver dust. She sprinkles the dust from one side of the shop window to the other, covering a few inches from the shop onto the sidewalk. She places the silver dust in a circle in front of the door. As she walks back inside and locks the door, across the way coming out of the alley, she sees the beast.

Nadia quickly runs back to her counter as the beast leaps quickly across the street and onto the sidewalk in front of the shop. Nadia grabs the gun from behind the counter and aims it at the front door. The beast snarls and slowly walks toward the door. Its eyes see the silver dust. It sniffs to see what it is, and quickly snarls and turns its head away. It growls in anger at Nadia. Nadia cocks the gun preparing to fire if necessary. The beast attempts to move forward, its foot hits the powder, and the flesh and hair begin to burn. It whimpers and growls, pulling its foot away, which is now badly burned. It growls again at Nadia and decides to retreat. The beast limps away back into the alley and out of sight. Nadia lowers the gun as it disappears.

Later that evening, at the edge of town, deep in the woods, Mazey opens a bottle of wine in the kitchen of a small wood cabin. She pops the cork. Takes a good size swig from the bottle and wipes her mouth. She carries the bottle into the living room and down the hall which is decorated with many frames of pictures of her and her dad, her mother, and family members. She stops and looks at a picture of her and her father, on the day she started with the Sheriff's office. Her father was a handsome man, with strong facial features, and a salt and pepper beard. She takes another swig from the bottle. "I'm going to find you, Dad!" She states to the picture. Underneath the picture is another framed photograph. This one is of Mazey and Riley from their high school graduation. She smiles at how young and innocent they were.

Mazey walks down the hall and to the basement door at the end. She enters the basement, flipping on the light and walks down the stairs. The basement feels like another living room. It is filled with a couch and table with two chairs. Bookcases fill one wall. The opposite wall has a small bar that appears to still be fully stocked. Mazey walks straight to the bookcases and makes her way to the far right. She reaches a hand behind the shelf, and with a little might, pulls the shelf open like a door. Behind the door is a small hallway about four feet long. At the end of the hallway is a large steel door with a wheel on the front of it. Two key holes on either side of the wheel. It looks like a giant safe. Mazey makes her way to the door. She lays the bottle of wine on the floor. From each pocket she pulls out two identical large keys, one of which is from Nadia's. She inserts the two keys into each hole next to the wheel. At the same time, she turns each key toward each other. A large click sounds from within the door. She grabs the wheel and spins it to the left till it stops. Three loud clicks sound from within the door. She removes the keys.

Mazey hits a small button on the wall which closes the bookcase. She pushes on the door, and it opens into a small room. She grabs the wine and walks into the room, flips a switch that turns on the lights, and she closes the door behind her. She spins the wheel that is on the back of the door until it stops, Three loud clicks sound, the door is locked. The small room is filled with boxes, books, and cork boards filled with maps and pictures of individuals, most of them in military uniforms. A large desk sits on one wall covered in papers, files, and a CB radio. Above the desk is a wall of monitors, which reveal every angle of the cabin both outside, and inside the cabin as well. On another wall is a large map of Forest River Hill and the National Park that surrounds it. Circled in a top corner of the map is a large region. Inside the circle is "AREA: FRH 41".

Mazey lays the wine on the table. She reaches on the floor and pulls a box onto the desk. She opens the lid to reveal papers and files. She searches through the box until she comes to a file, where the label reads "Cave Wolf." She pulls it out and opens it on the desk. Inside the folder is paperwork and a picture of her father, a young Howard Morehouse and a few of the local Indians. In between them is a dead wolf. The wolf is much larger than the average wolf you would see on a nature show. It is also covered in a dark thick fur and has large hands and feet. "Could we have another one of these roaming around?" she asks. She removes the picture from the file, folds it up and puts it in her pocket.

Mazey takes another swig off the wine bottle. She looks at the large map of the area on the wall. She spots a small area circled. Underneath the circle is written "behind the falls." Mazey's attention is drawn to a red light on one of the monitors, showing the front steps of the front porch. Mazey looks into the monitor and sees movement in the frame, It looks like the back end of an animal. She dismisses it and turns back to the file. She reads notes from her father in the file. "September 23rd, Dr Milton was picked up by MP's and taken to base. He was returned four days later. Became head of surgery at the end of October." Mazey

reads aloud. She flips through more papers, and near the end of the file

is a picture of the outside of Chaney's Woodshop and Taxidermy.

Mazey picks up the picture and looks at it.

"What did you stumble upon, pops?" Mazey asks aloud. She grabs the

wine and takes a pretty good swig. She looks around the room. It is

obvious her dad was looking into something and didn't want anyone to

know. "I know you left me a clue. Now where did you hide it?" She

asks aloud. On the wall she spots a piece of paper with one word on it

with two question marks, 'Hybridization??'

Chapter 20: Hypothetically

The crisp morning and the dew blanket the streets of downtown. The remanence of last night's festival still lingers along the sidewalks. Paul makes his way down the street toward Nadia's shop. He stops just outside her door as he notices the silver dust arranged along the front border of the shop. He spots what looks like a burned part of the concrete where the beast stepped. He knocks on the door even though the shop is still not open. Nadia emerges from the back and sees Paul. She slowly walks to open the door.

"Good morning deputy, how may I help you?" Nadia asks. "Sorry to come by so early, but I was hoping you had a few minutes. I have some questions about the book you gave me." Paul asks. Nadia looks at his eyes, she can see the concern in them. She also senses that he has had an encounter with the beast. "Absolutely, please come in." Nadia opens the door fully and allows Paul to come in. She closes and locks the door behind him. "Come back here, I'll pour you some coffee." Nadia says as she leads him to the back of the shop, through the curtain and into the back room with the books and weapons. She pours Paul a cup of coffee and hands it to him. Paul's eyes fixed on the weapon case and black bookcase he saw the first time he arrived.

"Now, what questions do you have for me?" Nadia asks. "You promise not to laugh at the silliness of these questions?" Paul asks. "No questions are silly deputy, I run a Lore store, remember?" Paul sips his coffee, feeling a little less nervous about what he is about to entertain.

"I read that book you gave me about Lycons, or werewolves. I grew up watching creature feature movies, and werewolf movies were some of my favorites. As I got older and realized the myth and legend of these stories and how fictitious it all was, I put those movies behind me. That book was a different version of those Hollywood stories. It read more like a history book, than a fun creature feature novel." Paul states. Nadia studies his expression, trying to discern what he wants from her. "That book was originally written in the second century. It was used as a genealogy of werewolf lines throughout the modern world that dated back a few thousand years before Christ was born." Nadia states.

"Are you saying this book is eighteen centuries old?" Paul asks. "The information is that old and has been added to all the way up to the newest edition of that book." Nadia answers him. "When was this version produced?" Paul asks. "That copy was published in 1940 by the Nazi Party. It was part of Hitler's private collection." Nadia states. "How did you come to possess it?" Paul asks. "My great grandfather was a curator for Hitler. When he knew the end was near and the war was over, he fled with the help of an American army captain. He took a collection of important books with him, and most are on that bookcase. The Lycons book was part of that collection." She informs.

"The book talks about a hierarchy of werewolves, almost like a military rank, based on age and ability. The generals change at will and produce a change in new Lycons." Paul states. "Are you asking these questions deputy out of interest, or have you seen something you need clarity on?" Nadia sternly asks. Paul pauses. He knows he has to tell someone. He was afraid to mention it to Mazey since he may lose his job for being crazy. "You know we are dealing with the attack in the National Park. It appears to be a large animal, but it also may be a man. A few nights ago, something came out of my woods behind the house that wasn't like anything I have ever seen before. Now, fair to say I had a few drinks that evening and some questionable fish, so I may have been tired and not in my right mind." Paul describes.

Nadia takes a moment and thinks about what she will say next. "If you are asking me deputy, if I think werewolves exist, my answer is yes. As long as the devil exists, many unnatural things will as well." Paul takes a deep breath of relief as if to believe he is not the only crazy one in town. "Are you worried that what you're dealing with in the park incident may be unnatural?" Nadia asks. "I'm hoping not. I'm hoping it is either a rabid animal or a disagreement among men. I have had a few strange incidents occur since I've been in town, so I just have more questions than answers." Paul states. Nadia is aware Paul is still holding back something. "Deputy, is there something hypothetically you want to know?" Nadia wisely asks. Paul smiles, knowing she is on to him.

"If we are talking hypothetically, then yes. Let's say in an alternate universe what we are dealing with in the park is a werewolf. If we were to come face to face with it, how could it be killed?" Paul asks. Nadia smiles, as this is what she lives for. "Well, deputy, hypothetically werewolves are immune to most things, and have incredible healing powers. There are two sure fire ways to kill a werewolf. You can behead it if you can get close enough and weald a powerful enough sword. The other way is to find a way to get pure silver in its blood stream. History has shown that silver is the better choice. There is only a half dozen records of beheadings." Nadia explains.

"So, the silver bullet isn't a myth?" Paul asks. "Not entirely." Nadia responds. "So, hypothetically, where can one get silver bullets around here?" Paul smiles as he poses this question. Nadia walks over to the case where the weapons are. Paul looks over at what she is pointing to. It is a large, all silver forty-four magnum six-shooter pistol, with diamonds on the handle. "That would do the trick." Nadia states. She opens a drawer under the case revealing multiple rows of forty-four caliber bullets. "Those are from a silver mine in Austria, and they would penetrate the thick hide of any werewolf, if they actually existed." Nadia suggests. She also grabs a bag and a small wand with a green amulet at the end of it. "If you need to slow the beast down, bang the wand on a hard surface. It will release a noise and light they do not like. You can also throw the dust in this bag on them, and it will agitate them for a few seconds, giving you enough time to aim and shoot." Nadia continues.

"So, hypothetically, if there was a werewolf anywhere near this town, that gun and bullets; the wand with the jewel, 'and' the bag of dust should do the trick?" Paul asks. Nadia smiles, as if to let Paul know they are his if he wants them. "Hypothetically!" Nadia states.

Chapter 21: I'm Kind of on Duty

The last day of the fall festival is upon us, and almost the entire town has shown up to enjoy the festivities and to create memories for years to come. As promised, Riley is escorting Paul through the festival, discussing all the major attractions the festival has to offer. She walks him over to a concession truck that reads "Hal's Heavenly Hops," owned and operated by Hal Ford, the local brewmaster of the town. Hal leans out the order window as he sees Riley and Paul come forward. "Riley Forest, so good to see your smiling face this afternoon." Hal happily states.

"Afternoon, Hal. Have you met our new deputy Paul Weather?" Riley asks. "I have heard the rumors and have been waiting to meet you sir." Hal extends his hand to shake. "So happy to have you part of the Forest River Hill family" Hal says. Paul extends his hand to shake Hal's. "Honor to serve this community, sir." Paul responds. "Whatever you want today, Deputy, it is my treat!" Hal states. Paul smiles in appreciation, "I really shouldn't, I'm kind of on duty." Riley, not having any of that, looks at Paul. "I won't tell Mazey, if you won't Hal." She remarks. "What she said!" Hal agrees. Paul smiles as if he will not put up much of a fight.

"Two Pumpkin-Maple Stouts Hal and give us the big cups." Riley requests. "You got it!" Hal obliges. Hal retreats to get the beers. "One beer, you'll be fine. You're a tall, strong, man." Riley jests. "When in Rome, right?" Paul smirks. "Exactly!" Riley agrees. Hal brings two large cups filled with his seasonal beer. They grab the cups. "Thank you so much Hal!" Riley says. "Come back for more if you like it. Stop by the brewery next week Deputy and I'll spot you a case of that if you like it." Hal states. "That sounds like a deal." Paul responds. Riley and Paul cheer to the beers and take a sip. Paul's face shines as the pumpkin-maple stout tastes amazing. "Wow!" Paul states, and nods to Riley for her good choice. "I'll take that free case, and will pay for another, Hal" Paul says. "You're on!" Hal responds.

Paul and Riley walk down the street, enjoying the beer and each other's company. Paul is taken by how pretty Riley is as the sun shines on her hair and face, her smile is warm and inviting. It has been so long since a woman has been in his life. He isn't sure he knows how to have these moments anymore. All he knows is that considering all the crazy, scary events that have happened in the last few weeks, today seems to make all of that less stressful. He is enjoying the walk, the time, and the emotions it is providing him. They approach Bigfoot's Café, where they have provided tables outside for people to enjoy the festival and the weather.

"You know what would go perfect with this beer? Our famous Bigfoot Cinnamon Rolls." Riley states as they make their way to the café. She points to a small empty table out front. "Grab us a seat there, I'll run in quickly and get us one." Riley says as she lays her cup on the table. She smiles at Paul as she heads inside. Paul sits down at the table and continues to drink his beer. He watches as people walk by, look at him and smile. Paul smiles back, enjoying the kind and festive atmosphere. It's a strong contrast between the death and darkness of the murders in the park. Paul looks across the street and notices a girl staring at him. It is Lia Anderson, the girl from Mazey's house the night the Mayor stopped by.

Paul stares back at her, and there is a strange connection as they look at each other. Lia smiles at him and waves. Paul returns the favor, smiles, and waves back. "Who are you waving at?" Riley asks as she comes to the table holding a large plate with a huge cinnamon roll on it. Paul, startled, turns away from Lia and looks at Riley. Riley sits down. "Waving at?" Paul asks. He looks back to Lia, but she is gone. He looks down the street to see her, but he cannot place her. He turns back to Riley, "Just some townsfolk being friendly." He states. "I bet you are super popular being the new guy in town and all." Riley jests.

Paul finally looks down at the enormous cinnamon roll, which definitely would feed four people. "You weren't kidding, that is huge!" Paul proclaims. "I know they say everything is big in Texas, but here in Idaho, we have some big things too!" Riley states. Paul picks up the fork and tries the cinnamon roll. The icing oozes off every inch of it, and the warm cinnamon sticks to the dough with every bite. Paul closes his eyes as the flavor touches every taste bud in his mouth. A large smile forms on his face. "Better than sex, right?" Riley asks.

Paul chuckles, as it has been a while since he experienced the other. "Probably. It's been a minute since the other, so my memory is failing me." Paul responds. "What a shame." Riley smirks back at him. Paul sips his beer to wash down the bite. "You were right though; this combination is heavenly." Riley smiles. She is glad Paul is finally enjoying a moment in this town. "So happy I can provide you with your first real Forest River Hill Fall Festival experience." Riley says. Paul wipes his mouth. "You certainly have. This is a memory I will keep for a long time hopefully." Paul remarks. Riley begins to enjoy the cinnamon roll as well. The two enjoy a few moments of silence as they enjoy the treats. They remain in as much eye contact as possible, growing fonder of this moment with each bite.

"Sorry you had to see 'the lawyer' side of me the other day, but Mazey tends to overstep her bounds with suspects." Riley remarks. "No, I understand. We all have a job to do, and it is not always pleasant or shine a pretty light on us." Paul responds. "I much prefer moments like this." Riley says. Paul smiles, agreeing this is a great moment. "In the heat of things, I'm sure I can be a bit of an asshole, especially to those I am throwing to the ground and handcuffing." Paul states.

"I'm sure most of the time they deserve it anyway." Riley adds. "Some people resist more than others. I guess I just have to be more persuasive." Paul smiles as he says. Riley gets the innuendo. "Speaking of that, can I still persuade you to enjoy a hayride later with me?" Riley asks. Paul smiles and sips on his beer. "A few more of these tasty beers and who knows what I will agree to." Paul jests. Riley laughs, enjoying the comfort of the conversation. "Is that so? Well maybe we need to return to 'Hal's Heavenly Hops' after we finish this cinnamon roll?" Riley suggests. Paul laughs as well. "Forget the hayride, if you and I finish this cinnamon roll and these beers, I'll need a wheel barrel to get me to the next block." The two laugh and enjoy the moment, understanding that there is a strong attraction between the two. Neither one wishes for this to be interrupted.

"Weather, this is Keller. Come in, over!" The moment is interrupted by Mazey through Paul's radio. The smiles fade on both their faces. Paul clicks his radio. "This is Weather's, over!" Paul responds. "Meet me at the station in five minutes. Ranger Evers has spotted Chaney's truck over near the town of Danbury, over!" Mazey states. "Got it. Five minutes, at the station, over!" Paul replies. Paul and Riley stare at each other, knowing their moment has ended. "I'm afraid we will have to finish this massive cinnamon roll another time. Sorry about that." Paul apologizes. "You were right, you were on duty, anyway. I promise I won't tell Mazey about the beer." Paul stands, Riley does as well. "I'll box this up. It goes really well with coffee. Maybe I'll swing it by the station tomorrow morning and we can finish our conversation." Riley says. "That would be great. I'll take a raincheck on the hayride as well." Paul responds. "You got it, Deputy." Riley adds. "Bye" Paul says softly. "Be careful." Riley responds back. He smiles and walks away. Riley sighs, upset their day ended so abruptly, but she is glad they had the moment.

Chapter 22: Country Strong

The sun is starting to set over the woods in the town of Danbury. On a country road Mazey and Paul slowly pull up to Ranger Evers and Officer Jackson as they flag them down on the side of the road. Ranger Evers' truck and Officer Jackson's squad car are parked up close to the tree line off the road. Mazey pulls her truck behind theirs and turns off the engine. Paul and Mazey join Evers and Jackson next to the woods. "What is the situation, Hocho?" Mazey asks. "I spotted Chaney's vehicle in the campground area of Beaver Lake State Park this morning. I waited till I saw him with my own eyes. I followed him here. There is a dirt road a half mile up that leads to an old cabin about four hundred yards through these woods. I know because this used to be owned by an old fur trapper who disappeared about ten years ago." Hocho states.

"Was he armed when you saw him?" Mazey asks. "I couldn't see anything on him, but he did have a couple rifles in his truck I could see. I called Officer Jackson, who I knew was in the area, right after I called you." Hocho responds. "Jackson, thanks for getting here to help."

Mazey says. "Yes ma'am" Officer Jackson responds. "Since we don't know if he is alone or not, and we are losing the light here in about an hour, let's spread out twenty yards apart and head toward the cabin. When we get there, Evers, you and Jackson swing around the back and wait for us to enter the front. As soon as you hear anything, make your way in through the back. Everybody got that?" Mazey asks. They all nod in agreement. "Let's grab rifles just in case we have to stay a distance from the house.

They each retrieve their rifles from the vehicles and begin walking through the woods. Twenty yards away from each other they make the trek through the thick brush, uphill, to the cabin tucked away. The light is slowly dimming as the sun disappears behind the mountainside. As they enter the final one-hundred yards the cabin comes in sight. A rustic, old, man-made cabin which appears to just have a few rooms. Thirty yards away from the cabin is a wooden barn, bigger than the cabin and chained shut. Several old cars are sprawled along the road to the cabin and amid the yard, acting as a barrier around the cabin. Mazey signals for them to stop about twenty yards before the forest ends. The men stop. She motions for Evers and Jackson to begin their route around the back of the cabin. Evers and Jackson quietly make their way to the back side.

Mazey signals Paul to meet her behind an old pick-up truck about twenty feet in front of the cabin. Paul and Mazey quietly make their way behind the truck. They perch themselves, rifles ready and peer over the edge of the pick-up bed into the small cabin. They can see a figure, tall and dark, walking between rooms through the dirty windows. The figure sits down at a table. The head can be seen now. It is Lonnie Chaney. Paul and Mazey recognize him. "That's him!" Mazey states. "Be two steps behind me and to the left. Be ready to fire if he has a weapon." Mazey states. "I've got your back." Paul responds. Mazey takes a deep breath, then moves from behind the truck and scurries to the front door. Paul, like a shadow right behind. They make it up the small steps and to the front door. Mazey stops, and Paul positions himself behind her as she requested. Mazey readies herself and then knocks on the door. "Mr. Chaney! Sheriff's department! Open the door!"

Inside the cabin, Lonnie sits at the kitchen table, in front of him is a plate with a large bloody steak on it. He looks up quickly with the knocking of the door. He takes a bite of his steak. Another knock at the door. "Mr. Chaney! Sheriff's department! Open the door or we will tear it down!" Mazey shouts. Lonnie pushes his plate aside in anger. His tall seven-foot frame stands, and he makes his way to the front door.

Evers and Jackson see Lonnie move to the front door and slowly make their way through the back door, on the back side of the kitchen. Lonnie slowly opens the front door. Mazey and Paul aim their guns straight at him. Their heads look up at the towering man. The door frame cuts off the top of his head. Lonnie is wearing overalls with a white shirt underneath, Mazey stairs at the blood stains on the shirt.

"Lonnie Chaney, I need you to take three steps back and turn around. You are under the arrest in suspicion of the deaths of Mark Roberts, Bill Molten and Larry Brett." Mazey loudly announces. Lonnie does not move. He stares at Paul and Mazey, his eyes deep and dark. "Lonnie Chaney, take three steps back! Turn around, put your hands on your head, and kneel down!" Mazey, again announces loudly to him. The three of them continue to stand, tense and nervous. Lonnie continues to stand and stare like a cold statue. He hears from the kitchen the sound of Jackson and Evers approaching. Lonnie quickly slams the door shut and rushes back into the kitchen. He quickly turns the corner and surprises Jackson and Evers.

With intense strength he knocks Jackson out of the way and knocks his gun out of his hand. Before Evers could aim at him, Lonnie knocks the gun out of Evers' hand, grabs his collar and raises his body up off the ground.

The front door bursts open as Mazey and Paul knock it down. They rush to the kitchen just in time to see Lonnie throw Evers into the back wall of the kitchen. His body slams hard against the wall and falls to the floor. Jackson reaches his feet and lunges after Lonnie pushing him into the stove. "Freeze! Put your hands behind your head, now!" Mazey shouts. Paul and she aim their guns at Lonnie. Jackson who is a big man himself, six-five, probably two-hundred and sixty pounds of muscle, holds Lonnie around the waist. Lonnie, with crazy strength pulls Jacksons' hands off his waist. He slams them on the stove.

Jackson pulls them back in pain. Lonnie grabs Jacksons' face and with a swift hard thrust, headbutts Jackson hard. Jacksons' body buckles and falls to the kitchen floor.

Lonnie turns to Mazey and Paul angrily. His breath is heavy and hot. His eyes stare intently at the two of them. "I will shoot you were you stand!" Turn around, put your hands behind your head. This is your last warning!" Mazey shouts again. Lonnie does not comply. He squeezes his fists in frustration. Mazey squeezes her finger a little tighter on the trigger, anticipating her need to fire is soon approaching. Lonnie leans forward to attack. Mazey locks her aim on his head to fire. Before anything could happen, from behind an iron skillet crashes against the back of Lonnie's' head. His eyes go limp, along with his body, and he falls forward, face first, onto the kitchen floor. Mazey looks up and sees Hocho holding the iron skillet behind him.

"That's a big son-of-a-bitch!" Hocho announces as his breathing slows down. Paul rushes over to Lonnie's limp body and handcuffs his hands behind his back. Jackson slowly comes to from the headbutt. He rises to his feet and sees Lonnie handcuffed on the ground. "Thanks,

Hocho. Are you okay?" Mazey asks. "Yeah. But that boy is country strong." Hocho responds. "That's for sure." Jackson remarks as he shakes the cobwebs off his fuzzy head. "Alright boys, let's pick this big, dumb, son-of -a-bitch up and put his ass in the back of my truck." Mazey states. She reaches for her keys and gives them to Paul. "Run and get the truck, pull it up here. Hocho, tie his legs together as well. Jackson, you ride with me, give Paul your cruiser keys. He can follow us back to the station. Hocho, I want you to call the forensics team and get them out here to sweep this place. We may have solved this campsite mystery today." The boys jump to Mazey's commands. She stares at Lonnie's large body lying on the floor.

Chapter 23: What Remains

The morning of Halloween has arrived in the town of Forest River Hill. The town prepares for the fever of children running about in costumes, tricking and treating their way to a sack full of candy. It is a crisp cool day, and it appears to be quiet and peaceful. Mazey, Paul, Hocho and Officer Jackson were able to secure Lonnie Chaney in the jail cell at the Sheriff's Department. Mazey and Paul pull up in her truck to Matt White's house just outside downtown. Mazey is interested in hearing Matt's story again about the campsite now having Lonnie's DNA and forensic evidence placing him there. They walk up to the front door. "His boss says he has not been to work in several days, and no word from him either. We may have a runner." Mazey states. She knocks on the door. "Sheriff's Department. Matt White, are you in there? Sheriff's Department!" Mazey shouts. They wait a beat for an answer, but none comes. She tries to open the door, but it is locked. "Go around the back to see if anything is open." Mazey tells Paul. Paul nods and heads around the side of the house. Mazey knocks again, "Matt White, Sherrif's Department. Open up!"

Paul walks around the house and up onto the back porch. His eyes immediately lock onto the dried throw up and blood on the back porch, and what looks like something being dragged through it. "Sheriff, you better get back here!" Paul announces on his radio. "Roger, on my way." Mazey responds. Paul kneels down to get a closer look. He looks at the back door and notices it slightly ajar. He stands and draws his weapon. Mazey comes quickly around the corner and sees the blood and puke as well. "What the hell happened here?" She asks. "Looks like someone or something was attacked and dragged out of the house." Paul states. Mazey looks at the back yard and the clear imprint in the grass of something being dragged along it. "Door is open." Paul states. Mazey signals Paul to go inside.

They slowly make their way inside. Some lights are on. Mazey signals Paul to go down a hallway and check the rooms. Mazey walks through the dining room and into the kitchen. The items Matt used to make his burger still remain on the counter. She looks around understanding Matt was here recently. She walks back into the living room as Paul comes back through the hallway. "It's clear, nobody home." Paul says. "It seems like someone was here yesterday or the day before, probably no more than three days ago I'd say." Mazey responds. "May want to

warn Jackson and Hart to be careful over at Al's." Paul suggests.

"Good call!" Mazey responds. She gets on her radio to warn the others.

"Jackson, come in. This is Keller, over."

"This is Jackson, over." Jackson responds on the radio. "Be advised, we

have strange activity over here at Matt White's house. No one is home,

but it appears the house has been abandoned. Be advised when

approaching Al Thorn's place, over." Mazey advises. "Roger that. We

are just pulling up now. Will proceed with caution, over." Jackson

responds. "Let me know what you find, over." Mazey responds and

looks at Paul. "I think we need to pay a visit to Joey Marx." Mazey

states. "I agree." Paul responds.

Across town, up the hill and through the woods, Officers Jackson and

Hart approach the front door of Al Thorn. When they notice the door

is slightly open, Jackson and Hart draw their weapons. "Al Thorn!

Sheriff's Department. We are coming inside." Jackson shouts as he

slowly pushes open the front door. Immediately he notices the dragged

blood on the floor of Al's entrance and living room. He also sees the ice cream stained on the floor and the television on. "Sheriff's Department!" Jackson announces one more time as he signals officer Hart to go around and check the other rooms. Jackson sees the side bathroom door open and the light on. He slowly makes his way to the bathroom, gun drawn, awaiting anything. He opens the door fully and steps in. He sees the bloodstains on the bathroom sink. "Hart!" He shouts. "All clear." She shouts back. Jackson leaves the bathroom and meets Hart back near the front door. "This doesn't feel right." Jackson states. "Definitely seems like there was an altercation here." Officer Hart replies. Jackson gets on his radio. "Sheriff, this is Jackson, over." He waits a beat. "This is Keller, over." Mazey responds. "Signs of an altercation here at Thorn's place. We have blood, and signs of abandonment of the house, over." Jackson says. "Roger that. Call May and have her send a team over to you and another team to Matt Whites house. We are on our way to Joey Marx place, meet us over there as soon as possible, over." Mazey responds. "Roger that, Sheriff. We are on our way, I'll call May in route, over." Jackson states, he motions Hart and the two of them exit Al's place.

Moments later, across town again in a small cul-de-sac Mazey and Paul stand outside Joey Marx's home. Jackson and Hart pull up and join them. The four of them huddle just outside Mazey's truck. "I spoke to Joey's work; he did not show up this morning." Mazey states. "What do think is going on here, Sheriff?" Officer Hart asks. "Nothing in this case has felt right from the beginning. I'm not sure what to expect as we walk in here. I'm hoping Joey is home sick, but he is not answering our calls. Weather and I will go in the front. You two go around the back just in case Joey or anyone else tries to run." Mazey states. Jackson and Hart nod and make their way around to the back. Mazey and Paul walk to the front door and knock. "Sheriff's Department! Joey Marx, are you home?" Mazey shouts. No answer. They wait a beat, then try again. "Sheriff's Department!" Still no response. Mazey turns to Paul. "Do you want to do the honors?" She asks. Paul smiles. "It's been a while, but it sounds like fun." Paul states.

"Sheriff's Department! We are coming in!" Mazey shouts. Paul takes a step back and with all his force drives his leg and foot at the front door. The force breaks the wooded frame on the side and the door opens. Mazey rushes in, gun drawn. Paul follows behind. "Not bad on your first try." Mazey jests. They look around. There seems to have been a disturbance here as well. Items have fallen on the floor and are out of place. "Joey Marx? Sheriff's Department!" Mazey announces one more time. Jackson and Hart come through the back door and dining room and join Mazey and Paul. "Back door was unlocked." Jackson states. Paul points to the floor leading down a hallway. Mazey turns and sees drops of blood leading to the primary bedroom.

She slowly follows the trail. Paul, Jackson, and Hart are close behind her. The blood spots get larger and larger as they lead into the primary bedroom. Spots turn into small pools as they enter the room. No sign of Joey. Mazey follows the blood trail as it leads to the bathroom. Small pools of blood become larger circles of blood and now pieces of flesh. Mazey aims her gun inside the bathroom and continues on. The bathroom tile is covered in blood, hair, and skin. The smell hits all of them. Paul covers his mouth, holding back the gagging. It is as Mazey feared. She enters the bathroom and to her worst fears discovers what appears to be Joey Marx, at least what is left of him, lying in the tub.

"Jesus Christ!" Mazey proclaims. She swallows hard and covers her mouth as she stares at the body of Joey Marx. Most of his legs and torso appear to have been eaten. What remains is mauled and gutted. His face was untouched, and the expression left only showed the terror and fear of what might have happened. Officer Hart turns away, hoping to forget what she has seen. Officer Jackson slightly coughs and gags. Paul stares intently, knowing that this was no man that did this. "Doesn't look like he was able to run away this time." Paul states.

Mazey turns away from the carnage. "Let's get a team here quickly and find out what happened. There has to be a clue from what remains." Mazey says. The terror rising in her eyes as she is unsure what is happening in her small town.

Chapter 24 Uncaged Animals

The full moon rises above Forest River Hill. The streets and neighborhoods are buzzing with trick or treaters as they finish up their rounds and gather as much candy as possible in their bags. Not participating in the festivities and alone at the Sheriff's Department is Paul. He sits at a desk in the back room where the jail cells are. He types away at the computer, finishing his reports from the incidents with Matt, Al, & Joey. Sitting on a bed in the large cell across from him is Lonnie Chaney. Lonnie watches Paul, his eyes fixed on his every move. "Weather, come in, over." The silence is broken by Mazey calling Paul on the radio. Paul ends his typing and responds on his radio. "This is Weather, over."

"I'm just finishing at the house, then I'm on my way over. How is our guest doing? Over." Mazey asks. Paul looks over at Lonnie who continues to eerily stare at him. "Quiet as a church mouse, over." Paul responds. "Alright, keep an eye out, I will be there shortly, over." Mazey responds. Paul stares at Lonnie, who stares right back. Paul looks to his side, on the floor next to him is a bag. Paul unzips the bag.

Inside is the 44-Magnum Silver gun Nadia gave to him, along with the bag of silver dust. He zips the bag back up. He sits back up and notices Lonnie has stood up and is standing just behind the cell's door. His head towers almost to the top of the cell. "You finally ready to make a statement?" Paul asks.

Lonnie looks the cell door over, running his large hands up and down the bars and the hinges. He turns back and looks at Paul. "You are going to make a fine addition to my pack." Lonnie finally speaks, his voice deep and gravely. Paul stands to his feet. He looks at Lonnie who now has a faint smirk on his face as if he is happy about something. Paul walks around the desk and up to the cell. He stands a couple feet away, puts his hand on his firearm and looks into Lonnie's eyes. "You don't like being in a cage big fella, do you?" Paul asks. "I've had my eye on you since you got here. I even visited you at the house one night." Lonnie states. Paul feels uneasy as Lonnie said that. He remembers the creature he encountered, hoping it was a dream or vision, but feeling more like it was real when Lonnie spoke. "I think all your animal stuffing has finally gone to your head." Paul responds. Lonnie leans his face into the bars of the cell door. "The only thing in my head tonight is what we are going to do to you and the Sheriff." Lonnie whispers.

Paul ponders what he said, then asks, "We?"

In that moment, one of the doors to the jail room opens. Paul turns, hoping to see Mazey walking in. To his surprise, walking through the door is Matt White and Al Thorn. Their clothes torn, bodies scraped and bloodied. They walk in the room almost in a trance. Paul quickly turns, recognizing who they are. He extends his hand to them. "Hold it right there gentlemen." Paul demands. Matt and Al continue to walk slowly towards him. Paul, hand still out, the other clutching his side arm, commands again, "I need both of you to turn around, put your hands behind your head." They continue to walk to Paul, silent and menacing. Paul takes a step back and begins to draw his weapon. Before he could do that two large hands grab him and forcefully slam him back against the cell. Lonnie has reached out and grabbed him. He forcefully holds his arms and torso against the cell.

"Don't fight it. You will only prolong the pain." Lonnie states. Matt gets close to Paul and grabs the cell door keys off his belt. Lonnie turns his head to the side, he opens his mouth wide, and a long tongue comes out and licks Paul on his neck. Al grabs Paul by the neck. Paul struggles to get free of Lonnie's strong grasp. "Let go of me you son-of-a-bitch." Paul struggles to say. Lonnie lets his grip go. Al takes Paul by the throat and his belt and hurls his body across the room and over the desk he was sitting at. His body crashes to the floor and passes out from the brutality of the throw.

"Come now, it is time." Lonnie says to Matt and Al. Matt unlocks the cell door. Lonnie walks back and allows the two to walk into the cell. Lonnie places his hands on Matt and Al's heads. "Let it be completed tonight." Lonnie states. Matt and Al begin to breathe heavily; they turn away from Lonnie and both get down on their hands and knees. Lonnie looks up to the ceiling and releases a loud howl. Matt and Al's bodies begin to morph. They scream and moan in pain as their limbs crack and expand. Their shoulder cracks out of joint and moves back. Their spines enlarge along with their facial features.

Paul comes to behind the desk and hears the sounds coming from the cell. He stands up to see the three men in the cell morphing into beasts. Lonnie quickly grows fur all over his body, which enlarges and expands, and it even appears as if he was growing taller. His ears enlarge and touch the ceiling. Matt and Al finish their transformation and become wolf-like beasts. Lonnie finishes as well and hovers over them. The three large beasts completely fill the cell. Paul frantically reaches over to the bag on the floor and pulls out the bag of dust and the silver gun Nadia gave him.

As he does one of the beasts leaps over on top of the desk. His ferocious mouth growls and drools over Paul. The beast swats at Paul with one of his paws, barely missing him. Paul quickly reaches into the bag and grabs whatever dust he can. The beast readies itself to leap onto Paul. Paul throws the dust into the beast's face. Smoke rises from the beast's face as it cries and yelps. The dust burning all it touches. The beast jumps off the desk and scurries away. Paul grabs the bullets from the bag and quickly loads the gun.

The other beast leaps at Paul from the side. Paul quickly reacts and jumps on the desk, barely avoiding the beast. He jumps from the desk and makes his way to the middle of the room. Paul turns and aims the silver gun at the beast in the corner. It turns and jumps on the desk, growling at Paul. Paul puts his finger on the trigger and begins to squeeze. However, before he could get off a shot Lonnie back hands Paul in the chest and knocks him back onto the floor. Lonnie stands over Paul. Frightening and intimidating. The hurt beast recovers and walks over to Paul on the floor, along with the other beast as it leaps from the table and comes to Paul. The three beasts now hover over Paul, snarling, waiting to strike. One puts its large paw on Paul's arm so he cannot raise the gun. Paul cringes in pain as one of the others climbs on his chest and right up to his face. The drool dripping on Paul's chin. The beast on his chest shows Paul the sharp row of teeth in its mouth and goes to bite Paul in the neck.

Bang! A shot is fired. The bullet hits the beast in the shoulder. It yelps and tumbles off of Paul. The burnt beast snarls and turns. Lonnie turns around and standing inside the back door is Mazey. Her gun drawn and ready. Her first shot saved Paul. Lonnie growls and charges after her. Bang! Another shot rings out. The bullet hits Lonnie in the shoulder and he stumbles backward. The burnt beast begins to charge and Mazey fires upon it, hitting it in the chest and knocking it to the ground. Lonnie turns back to Mazey. She keeps her aim. "Die, you big ugly bastard!" She says as round four is fired onto Lonnie's chest.

Lonnie is knocked back but not down. He looks down at the wounds in his shoulder and chest and seems more annoyed than hurt.

Lonnie glares back at Mazey who is in shock that the bullets have had no effect on the beast. Before she could fire all her rounds, in a flash Lonnie leaps at her, knocking the gun away and grabbing her. He lifts her body off the ground and brings her face up to his snout. Mazey tries to struggle but Lonnie's strength is too much. She stares into those evil eyes of his and understands what could have happened to those men in the woods and ultimately Joey at his house. Lonnie opens his mouth showing his sharp teeth and lunges for Mazey's face.

Suddenly the room is filled with a bright green flash and a high-pitched noise. Lonnie yelps in pain and lets go of Mazey. He holds his ears and whimpers into the middle of the room. Standing in front of the other doorway is Nadia. She is holding the wand with the glowing green stone on top. She bangs the wand on the wall again and another green flash and piercing noise fills the room. Lonnie snarls. The other two beasts cower on the floor holding their ears. "Get up!" Nadia yells at

Paul. Paul gets up and rushes over to Mazey as she lays on the floor in pain. Lonnie walks toward Nadia and stares at her. She engages with the beast, and they lock eyes on each other. Nadia showing no fear toward the giant beast. "Hagazussa" Lonnie says to her in a deep voice. Calling her in old German a Witch Spirit.

Nadia attempts to bang the wand again but Lonnie lunges at her and grabs her neck quickly, banging her body against the wall. The wand falls from her hand. He raises her body up to his face. He turns her head from side to side. Nadia now fearing for her life. Lonnie begins to squeeze her neck, choking the life from her. From behind Lonnie a gun cocks. Lonnie quickly turns to see Paul standing in the middle of the room. The silver 44-magnum pointed directly at him. Lonnie releases his grip and lets Nadia's body fall to the floor.

"We weren't finished, asshole!" Paul states. Lonnie snarls. The two other beasts rise and position themselves next to Lonnie. Lonnie points to the bullet wound in his shoulder and the other one in his chest. Lonnie snarls at Paul and points to another spot on the other shoulder as to tell Paul to shoot him there. Paul smiles. "Time for you to return to hell." Paul claims. He fires, the sound is fierce and loud as the silver bullet pierces Lonnie's shoulder knocking the beast back into the wall and to the floor. The wound sizzles, bubbles and burns as the silver penetrates the blood stream.

The two other beasts run after Paul to attack. Bang! Bang! Each shot dead center in their heads. They fall to the floor as the silver begins to burn their blood. Lonnie lifts his body up. He looks at the wound which is burning away the hair and flesh around it. He howls, snarls, and attempts to run toward Paul. Bang! The bullet hits dead center in Lonnie's chest. The power knocks him back. Lonnie recovers, sees the second wound and the damage it is doing. With one final attempt, Lonnie lunges at Paul. Bang! The next shot pierces Lonnie between the eyes dropping him to the floor. Paul, in pain and in shock, lowers the gun and falls to his knees.

Mazey makes her way over and checks on him. "Jesus, Paul, what the hell were those things?" She asks. "And where the hell did you get that gun.?" Nadia walks over to the two of them. "What in the hell was that flash and that sound?" Mazey asks her. Nadia grabs the gun from Paul's hand. "Some things are not explainable, Sheriff." Nadia says. "Not everything in this world is evil, but many things are." Nadia puts the gun in her bag. She then walks behind the desk to retrieve the bag of dust. Mazey and Paul stare at the bodies and are more distraught as they witness the beasts slowly changing their form. They were losing their hair and wolf-like features and in a moment, the jail room was filled with the dead naked bodies of Lonnie, Matt, and Al.

Nadia comes back around to them, putting the bag of silver dust in her bag as well. Mazey and Paul look up at her. "I would advise the two of you to try and get some sleep tonight, even if it is ten minutes. When you awake try to imagine all of this was a dream, or at the very least consider it what I call "Lore." Nadia says as she gives them a cheshire cat smile and walks out of the room. Mazey and Matt sit on the floor, both stunned, and staring at the bodies. Paul turns to Mazey. "Case solved?" He asks. Mazey can't help but to laugh. Between the chaos, insanity, terror, and absurdity of what just transpired, her instinct isn't to answer but just to laugh. This makes Paul giggle as well. Neither one is ready to grasp or understand these events. They are hoping Nadia is right and tomorrow this will all be a dream.

Chapter 25: The Morning After

It couldn't be a more beautiful morning, after such a horrific night. Paul sits on the steps of the back porch peering out into the lawn, the river, and the forest. His wounds are still fresh. His mind is still in shock. The warm coffee fights off the cool, crisp morning. A sound coming from his left disturbs the silence. He quickly looks, anticipating anything. His nerves calm as he sees Mazey coming around the side of the house. "I guess you didn't hear me knocking." Mazey says as she walks toward Paul. She brought fresh coffee and a bag of Danish as a gift. She hands Paul the coffee and the bag. "You can never have enough coffee. The bag is from Riley. It's a cinnamon roll." Mazey states. "You mind if I sit?" She asks. Paul smiles and scoots over on the steps. Mazey places her coffee down and sits next to him on the stairs. They both enjoy the view for a moment.

"I'm sure neither one of us is ready to talk about what happened last night, or even admit that last night actually happened. I was hoping to wake up on the floor somewhere with an empty bottle of whiskey next to me, praying it was a bad dream." Mazey breaks the silence. "I've seen some strange things in my life and stared down a few demons in my day. Whatever that was, is on a whole different level." Paul responds. "I'm sure you have a thousand questions. I wish I felt that I could answer them all. The truth is I've lived my whole life in this strange town, and I'm still not used to the unusual things that occurred." Mazey states. Paul sips his coffee, and chuckles to himself. "I wasn't a random hire, was I?" Paul questions. Mazey smiles, she turns to look him in the eye.

"Not exactly. I wasn't sure when I was going to tell you. Before my father disappeared, he was looking for you. We had a few conversations about you. He advised me that if anything happened to him, and things became difficult, that I was to find you and ask you to work for me here at the Sheriff's Department. He never really explained why, he would just always tell me that you had a calling on your life, and that calling would lead you here." Paul, listening to what she is saying, stares out at the flowing creek. He ponders if God has something strange in store for him. "So, what are you really trying to tell me?" He asks.

Mazey confesses about what she knows. "Two years before my dad disappeared, he spent hours investigating the military base which he came to know as 'AREA FRH41'. He had a theory, which most believed was a conspiracy theory, that this base was doing ungodly genetic experiments. Most of his colleagues, including the Mayor began to question his sanity. They began a campaign to remove him from the office. The main obstacle was that the people of Forest River Hill loved my dad. He was strategically warned by the military to end his inquiries. My dad knew though that every strange thing that has occurred in this town began when the base was opened in 1941. He called me one morning, said he found something, and he wanted me to meet him at his cabin." Mazey pauses for a moment, becoming emotional. "That was the last time I heard his voice. He wasn't at the cabin. He wasn't at home or at the station. He went missing. I did everything I could to get access into the military base. When they finally threatened my children, I stopped asking." Mazey wipes her tears.

"I stopped looking because my mother asked me too. I can still feel his presence sometimes, as if he is out there, somewhere. Maybe they threatened my life, and he left so nothing would happen. What I do know is this town has never been normal, and as long as that base is there, nothing is going to change." Mazey remarks. Paul was finally starting to get a sense of the purpose he might serve in his new role as deputy.

Across town, in the morgue of the hospital, Colonel Riser and a group of soldiers storm their way into the casket room. Dr Harrison, the head mortician, is stunned at the intrusion. Colonel Riser hands him a piece of paper. "You will notice that is the seal of the President of the United States, just below the signature of the president himself." Riser states. Harrison looks the paper over. "That is an executive order to retrieve the bodies of Matt White, Al Thorn, and Lonnie Chaney. Please advise the numbers on the caskets where these bodies are in." Riser demands. Harrison, still in shock, stares at the Colonel. "Now, sir!" Riser shouts. Harrison, now intimidated, "Uh, 17, 19 & 34." He shakenly responds. The soldiers quickly retrieve the bodies. They open the bags and use a small device to scan the faces of the bodies to confirm they are correct. "The United States Military thanks you for your patriotic cooperation! Have a good day, sir!" Riser says as he turns and leaves the morgue. The soldiers, with body bags in hand, follow closely behind.

Back at Paul's they're interrupted suddenly by May. "Sheriff Keller, this is May, come in. Over." "This is Keller, over!" Mazey responds. "You're needed at the morgue. Dr. Harrison called. He said the military came in and took the bodies. Over," May announces. Mazey and Paul look at each other. Their conversation coming to light. "Roger, May. We will head that way. Over."

"So much for it being a dream." Paul states. Mazey looks Paul in the eyes. She knows this is the moment where she will be alone or have a real partner to solve these mysteries. "I will completely understand if you want to turn in your badge, pack your bags, and get the hell out of this town right now. I'm sure when you filled out that application for the Deputy position there was not a section asking if you have worked with monsters before. If this is not for you, now is the time to let me know." Mazey states.

Paul sees that she is serious about understanding how crazy all this is. "What, and miss all the fun? I spent my childhood reading monster stories. I sailed the world fighting terrorists. I studied the occult and the paranormal and spent hours battling demonic forces. No, I think I'm exactly where I'm supposed to be." Paul responds. Mazey smiles, hoping that would be his response.

"I'm happy to hear that, partner. I'm glad I have a soldier like you fighting this battle with me." Mazey stands to her feet and extends her hand to help Paul up. "Let's find out what happened to our werewolves!" Mazey states. Paul smiles, but shakes his head, still in disbelief of all that has transpired. Paul gives her his hand as she helps him to his feet. They both sip their coffee and stare out at the creek and the forest that lies beyond.

Paul looks around at the house and smiles. "This place could use a few upgrades. Is it too early to ask for a raise?" Paul smiles as he says it. Mazey smirks, then walks into the house.

Chapter 26: AREA FRH41

Through the forest, over hills, dirt roads and into the National Park, following the trails winding passed the police taped campsite, and to the edge of the fence where the beast deposited his victim, lies the military base. Large military vehicles drive down the roads that surround the four-story building which is the width of a football stadium. It is secured on all sides by armed soldiers and guarded towers. Inside this secured, top-secret base is an automated guarded door that protects a multitude of winding corridors ultimately leading to a large elevator which is labeled *"AREA: FRH41"* that only "top secret" clearance will open. The elevator leads to a subterranean level which contains a dimly lit corridor with rooms on either side. A soldier holding a tray of food walks to a vault-like steel door on the left marked "D425". There is a small window and lower small-flapped drawer in the center of the steel door revealing a small room. The soldier opens the small drawer and places the tray of food inside and quickly closes it. He turns and briskly walks back down the corridor.

A man sitting at a small desk against the wall within that room stops writing on his piece of paper and stands slowly. His long hair and beard cover most of his appearance and his attire is somewhat ratted and torn. As he gets closer to the tray, a little weathered and a few years older, Mazey's father, the missing former Sherrif Keller, rapidly consumes his rations graciously provided by his captors.